A Bone from
a Dry Sea

By the same author:

A Bone from a Dry Sea

a Dry Sea

PETER DICKINSON

Delacorte
Press

Published by
Delacorte Press
Bantam Doubleday Dell Publishing Group, Inc.
666 Fifth Avenue
New York, New York 10103

This work was first published in Great Britain in 1992 by Victor Gollancz Ltd.

Library of Congress Cataloging in Publication Data

Dickinson, Peter [date of birth]
    A bone from a dry sea / by Peter Dickinson.
      p.   cm.
    Summary: In two parallel stories, an intelligent female member of a prehistoric tribe
becomes instrumental in advancing the lot of her people, and the daughter of a
paleontologist is visiting him on a dig in Africa when important fossil remains are
discovered.
    ISBN 0-385-30821-3
    [1. Man, Prehistoric—Fiction.   2. Paleontology—Fiction.   3. Fossils—Fiction.]   I.
Title.
  PZ7.D562Bn   1993
  [Fic]—dc20   92-20491
                                                    CIP
                                                    AC

Manufactured in the United States of America

March 1993

10   9   8   7   6   5   4   3   2   1

BVG

Myth in all tongues credits the dolphins with
Making the bays they visit happy, waking
Song in flint cottages that lacked it long.
Man haunts what shores he can.

Then

The child clung to the rock, letting the broken waves of the bay wash over her, cooling the fierce sunlight. She was not afraid. The sea was her home.

Light dazzled off the water, but she kept her head above the surface and gazed steadily toward the mouth of the bay. She was on shark watch. Out on the open shore grown males would keep watch, but a submerged rock shelf barred the entrance to this bay, so it was safe to let the children learn the duty.

She was hungry. For days now the wind had blown hard from the southeast, driving the ocean rollers before it. The tribe used the bay because there were caves in the low cliffs, deep in two of which fresh water trickled down the rock. But food inside the bay was scarce, so normally they would have hunted the rocky inlets beyond for shellfish and shrimp and crabs and the little octopi that hid under boulders.

But with a wind like this the dark green rollers pounded in, hurling their foam to the clifftops and then dragging anything loose back seaward in their weight of water. Anyone who tried to feed out on the open shore would be swept away to where the sharks cruised, or break an arm or leg, or crush a foot. So by now all the tribe were hungry.

A hand touched the child's flank beneath the water. She glanced down, grinned a greeting as her mother rose beside her, and returned to her watch. Her mother had brought her two mussels, barely the size of a fingernail. Her mouth watered as she heard the crack of shells being pounded open, and she was putting her hand down to take them when she froze, pointed, yelled the warning *Big wave,* and immediately added the snapped-off hoot that meant *Shark!*

When each roller reached the submerged shelf at the bay's mouth it rose to a wall, ridged with foam, and seemed to hang for an instant before it crashed into the bay. In that moment before wave break the sun lit it from beyond. Now a giant wave, two waves in one perhaps, had come. It seemed to rise as high as the cliffs behind the bay and then poise at the entrance for longer than an ordinary wave. In its green-lit depths hung a darker, curving shadow as big as four grown males. Then it crashed down and its foam creamed over the bay.

The noise was enough to startle even people used to the surprises of the sea, so many of the tribe surfaced to look. The child was standing on the rock now, pointing and yelling. Her mother was racing for the shore. As the wave thunder died and before the next wave crashed in, they heard that the yell was *Shark!,* but mostly stayed where they were—it was only a child, mistaken, probably, or mischievous. Then the mother reached the shore and joined in the cry, and the whole tribe streamed for safety.

The shark had vanished. It must have been swimming along the shoreline, hunting perhaps for someone desperate enough to go foraging out in the open, when the monster wave had picked it up, a moving mass of water too powerful for it to be able to fight its way against, and so it had been tossed into the bay.

The child yelled again and pointed with her web-fingered hand. She had glimpsed the long shadow gliding beneath the ruffled surface a few paces from her rock. A moment later the dorsal fin broke the surface as the rising sea bed forced the shark upward.

The people yelled. The shark veered along the shoreline through a spatter of hurled rocks, and away down into deeper water. It vanished for a while but circled around by the rock again, and again the child yelled and pointed, and again the fin emerged. This time the people were ready, and larger rocks hailed around it. And again. And again.

At first they were trying to drive it away so that they could return to the water, but soon they realized it was trapped. Except in the moment when a wave came pounding in, the entrance to the bay was too shallow for it to pass. So now the tribe were the hunters and the shark the prey, if they could find a way to kill it. They spread along the shore harrying it on.

The child watched from the rock. Now that her eyes understood what they were seeing she could trace the shark's movements all around the bay, except through the turmoil at the entrance. She turned steadily, one arm raised to point, helping the others follow the track of their enemy. They surged along the shore, leaping from rock to rock, hurling anything they could lift. Cushioned by water few of these missiles can have hurt the shark much, but it grew half mad with fright and began to break from its circuit and make dashes across the bay, sometimes actually rubbing against the rock where the child stood. She kept to her task, unalarmed.

A shark must swim to keep water moving through its

gills, or it will die, so this one couldn't lie in the deep center of the bay, out of the tribe's reach. Around and around it had to go, enduring their attack. Now they grew bolder, some dashing into the water as it went by, with rocks in their hands to pound at the passing flank. These blows too did little damage, but the sense of dominance increased, infecting them all. Excited young males ran into the water ahead of it, ready for their attack. The cliffs echoed with the tribe's yells.

On the far side of the bay a male plunged in and followed the shark's path toward the rock. It looked like more bravado, but when he reached the rock he climbed out and stood beside the child. He was her uncle, a senior male, already beginning to challenge the aging leader, and he was taking this chance to increase his prestige by directing the shark hunt. He watched the shark make two more circuits while the child pointed its path, but next time, as soon as it was safely past the rock, he grunted *Go away* and pushed her into the water. She swam quickly ashore, glad to be out of the sun and free of the ache of pointing all the time.

She didn't join the others along the shoreline, but climbed to a patch of shade beneath an overhang, where she could sit and watch the hunt, while the tribe dashed in and out of the water, screaming and smiting, and beating the surface into gouts of spray. She alone seemed not to be swept up into the frenzy. She wanted to see.

A wild yell rose, on a different note, not rage or excitement, but pain. Those in the water rushed ashore. Two of them dragged a third. Blood streamed down his side. His left arm was missing, almost to the shoulder. The shark had attacked. Hunter and hunted had changed places again.

Sharks can smell blood a long way off. They race toward its source. The odor drives them mad.

All its terror forgotten, the killer threshed around the bay. It sensed the male on the rock and circled below him. It drove its snout into the air almost to his feet. Then it broke off and dashed toward the place where the water reeked most strongly. Though they were safe on shore the tribe scattered before it.

Quietly the child watched. There was no answer, she saw, until either the shark died or escaped. For it to escape there must be a big tide and no wind. But the tribe were also trapped until the wind dropped. And now they couldn't even forage for the scant pickings in the bay. Unless they could kill the shark they would starve before it did.

Out of nowhere the answer came into her mind.

The shark's mad rushes had a pattern. It surged toward the patch of blood-tainted water, found nothing there, sensed the live meat on the shore and slid along beside it, then remembered in its slow brain about the other meat, trapped on the rock, almost in reach, and hurtled out there, circling for a while until a waft of blood smell drew it on another frenzied rush toward the shore.

It had found its victim below and to the left of where the child was sitting. Here a ridge of rock sloped down into the water and became the bar at the mouth of the bay, with a wide shelf running beside it for some distance below the surface. It had caught its prey in the corner between the shelf and the shore. This was the place it made for each time.

Unnoticed the child made her way down to the water's edge and waited, watching the fin circle the rock. The snout nuzzled up toward her uncle. The toothed mouth gaped. Then the fin came slicing through the water toward her. She ran down onto the submerged shelf to meet it.

The tribe screamed. The shark saw her. The fin curved

from its path, heading straight at her. At the last instant she flung herself aside.

All her life, since she could paddle, she'd played catch-as-catch-can in and out of the water. She knew what she could do, but hadn't realized the shark's speed and power. If its charge hadn't been slowed by the slope of rock, it would have caught her. As it was she was knocked flat by the rush of its attack, which carried the streamlined body on up the slope right to the water's edge where it lay stranded, its gills in the air, its tail thrashing at the shallows behind it.

Gabbling and calling, the tribe gathered to watch it die. The child's uncle came swimming across to stand with one foot on the still-twitching body, shouting triumph and punching his fists into the air, as if it had been he who'd steered it onto the rock and killed it. The tribe shouted *Praise*. Gulls gathered above, joining their screams to the racket.

Without tools, apart from the stones they used to break crabs and shellfish open, it took time for the tribe to gnaw and claw their way through the tough skin of the belly, but they did it in the end. Their leader wanted to organize the sharing out of meat, but the child's uncle outfaced him and drove him back, taking the honor himself, allotting big pieces of liver to senior males and the mothers of newborn young. Then the families squabbled around the carcass, but without anger because they could see there was enough for everyone. Even the children slept that night with crammed stomachs.

The child who had watched from the rock got her share. Her mother had cuffed her for her stupidity and she had whimpered *Sorry* because that was expected of her, but as she lay among the crowded bodies in one of the caves, unable to sleep because of the mass of meat inside her, she relived the adventure. She knew what she had done, and why. She understood that it had not been an accident. She realized too that the others would not understand.

She had no words for this knowledge. Thought and understanding for her were a kind of seeing. She showed herself things in her mind, the rock shelf, the shallow water, the need to lure the shark full tilt onto the slope so that it would force itself out too far, and strand, and die; then her uncle triumphing and her mother scolding and herself cringing while she hugged her knowledge inside her.

Now she seemed to herself to be standing apart in the cave, seeing by the moonlight reflected from the bay one small body curled among the mass of sleepers. A thought which had neither words nor pictures made itself in her mind.

Different.

She's different. Yes, I'm different.

Now:
Sunday Morning

The truck wallowed along the gravelly road, if
you could call it a road. Often there was nothing to
mark it off from the rest of the brown, enormous
plain, but Dad knew where he was because then
there'd be tire ruts making the truck wallow worse
than ever. Vinny clutched the handgrip on the dash
to stop herself being thrown around. They'd done
two hours from the airport, though it seemed
longer, when Dad stopped by a flat-topped tree
with a lot of grassy bundles hanging among the
branches. Weaver birds, Vinny guessed. She'd seen
them on TV.

"Ready for lunch?" he said.

"I'm starving. How much further?"

"We're a bit over halfway. But look."

He pointed and Vinny stared through the shim-
mer of heat. Far off there were blue hills. Much
nearer something moved, changed shape, vanished
as the wavering air distorted the distance, and then
was there again, steady for a moment, three long,
slightly arching necks with small heads. She'd

known them since she was tiny, from the Noah's Ark frieze around her room.

"Giraffes," she said.

"Right."

"Are there any lions?"

"They'll be resting till it gets a bit cooler. Take a good look. We don't get much wildlife around the camp, because we're on the edge of the badlands."

"Why's it all so flat?"

"Because it was sea until a few million years ago. Those hills used to be the shoreline. In fact the section the camp's on seems to have been an island. Seen enough?"

He drove into the shade of the tree and fetched crates from the back of the truck for them to sit on while Vinny unpacked the lunch. Potato chips, Coke, chicken sandwiches, mangoes, and a Mars bar.

"I hope that's the sort of thing you like," he said.

"I like anything."

She sensed that he was as nervous as she was. They hadn't seen each other for over a year, and never before like this. It had always been London hotels, visits to the zoo or the planetarium, jerky talk about school and her friends and what she liked doing, both of them jumpy with having to watch what they said, because of the anger between him and Mom, still there, still no better, eight years after the split.

He ate in silence. Vinny was ready for this. That was one of the things Mom couldn't cope with, his silences. Whole days sometimes, she'd said. A complete skiing holiday once. The obvious thing was to be silent too, but Mom wouldn't have known how. Mom would be at Grasse by now, she thought, maybe at this very moment carrying the lunch tray out onto the terrace, talking as she came, Colin lounging in the vine shade with a tumbler of wine in his fist, the boys playing their dragon game among the olive trees below . . .

The cooling engine clicked. The weaver birds accepted the human presences and began to move and chatter. An ant the size of a button was dragging away a crumb of bread.

"You're not tired?" he said for about the fifth time.

"I'm fine. But listen, Dad—it's going to be all right, me coming. And if it isn't, then it's my fault. It was all my idea."

"So I gathered. Your mother . . ."

He didn't try to keep the sourness out of his laugh.

"Colin talked her into it," she said. "It makes going to Grasse a lot easier for them, you see—they don't have to bother about what I want, only them and the boys. You know, Mom was still trying to make me join an Outward Bound course or something till you said we couldn't go on a safari after all because you'd got to go on working, and you thought I'd be bored. That made it all right."

"Because it was a nuisance for me?"

"Not just that. She wouldn't mind so much provided I *was* bored. Look, Dad, I'll tell you what I think about Mom and then we don't have to talk about it anymore. It's a bit like Grandad and his bad leg—you know, there're things he just can't do because of it, but otherwise he's the same as anyone else. Only with Mom it's inside her. She just can't be sensible about anything to do with you. Apart from that she's the same as my friends' moms. She can be lovely, she can be a pain in the neck, you know? I'm lucky she fell for Colin. I really like him. The boys can be pests, but that's the age they are. But honestly, I'm a lot happier at home than some of the kids I know. You needn't worry —I'm not going to try and sucker on to you from now on."

"You've thought it all out?"

"Yes. I suppose I'm like that."

He grunted and went into another of his silences. Vinny ate the half-melted Mars bar, quite wrong for Africa but she knew he'd got it because she'd asked for one on a bitter winter day in London once. She glanced at him out of the corner of her eyes. Not like a dad, somehow, short, broad-chested, round-faced, dark-haired once but now more than half bald.

"It doesn't always work," he said.

"Uh?"

"Thinking things out. Oy oy—we're going to have to move. This lot are biters."

Out of nowhere troops of shiny orange ants had appeared, obviously intending to carry off not just the crumbs and leavings but the untouched food as well. Vinny helped pack up and climbed into the truck. Dad got in the other side but didn't start the engine.

"That's a good image of yours," he said. "Pop's bum leg, I'm talking about. You've got your head screwed on . . . Look, I'd better explain one or two things about the set-up at the camp."

"I thought I'd just keep my mouth shut till I found out."

"Still, it'll be easier if . . . Things aren't too good, you see. For a start, we haven't been lucky in our finds. That's always a risk. Any expedition has its ups and downs—you go a few weeks without significant finds and everyone gets short-tempered and bitchy—it's been such an effort to get here and you don't get that many chances, so you feel you're wasting your time, and the food tastes foul and stupid accidents begin to happen. But then someone comes up with something really worthwhile and everybody's on a

high, and they start seeing things they'd missed, and meals
don't matter . . . you understand?"

"You haven't found anything?"

"Not much. Some badly smashed fragments of one
skull. Hundreds of pig mandibles which might be useful
for dating if we'd found anything else of interest, which we
haven't. We've got plenty of material, but almost nothing
new. Joe's famous luck seems to have deserted him."

Vinny looked at him. The sour note was back, the one
he used when he was talking about Mom. She knew from
Dad's letters that Joe was Dr. Hamiska, who was leading
the expedition.

"You'd better know," he said. "Joe and I haven't hit it
off. Don't worry—he'll turn on the charm for you, all
right. But it's different with me. I was afraid this might
happen—in fact I was in two minds about joining the expedition in the first place."

"Why did you, then?"

"Partly personal reasons—you'll see. Maybe . . . But
from a professional point of view it was a terrific opportunity. There's been a civil war going on here for the last
twelve years and nobody's been able to get in. This is the
obvious next place to look for early hominid remains. Everyone I know has been itching to come, but things aren't
really settled down yet and the new government doesn't
want a lot of foreign paleontologists poking around, so
they have turned everyone down—except, of course, Joe
Hamiska. Absolutely typically he had a line to the Minister
of the Interior, through an ex-pupil who happened to be
the Minister's nephew. You'll meet him. He can't stop
talking. So here we are, in one of the hottest, dreariest bits
of Africa, with this unique opportunity to increase the sum
of human knowledge, and not getting anywhere. Do you
understand?"

"I think so. Why's it the obvious place to look?"

"Did you read any of those books I suggested?"

"Oh, yes. All the ones I could find in the library."

"Good for you. Then you'll know there's an enormous gap in the fossil record of human evolution?"

"You'd better remind me."

"Well, about ten million years ago there were apelike creatures, walking on four legs and so on, and just enough to show that they're probably our ancestors, and then there's a huge gap to about three and a half million years ago when there are creatures something like us, with smaller brains than ours but walking on two legs and with jaws much nearer to ours and so on. Between those two points there's one doubtful tooth and one even more doubtful bit of jaw. Now, if you look at a map of Africa and plot the various finds this side of the gap, and their probable dates, you'll find you've got a rough line running northeast. Start at the newer finds, carry on through the older finds and on a bit further, and you finish up here. Right?"

Vinny gazed around the stretching distances.

"There's still an awful lot of places to look," she said.

"That's where Joe's famous luck comes in. There's exactly one Western-educated paleontologist in the country."

"The Minister's nephew?"

"Right. He came to Joe with a bit of pig jaw someone had brought in. Pigs are important, because they evolved in a nice simpleminded way and if you know your stuff you can date their jaws pretty accurately, and then you've got a good idea that anything you find alongside them is likely to be roughly the same date. This bit of jaw turned out to be between four and five million years old. Reports of plenty of other fossils around. You see?"

"I'm not surprised you wanted to come."

"It was touch and go. A lot of good people turned Joe down when he asked them to join."

"And now you wish you had too?"

"Well, it's not entirely Joe's fault. In some ways the place has turned out to be a paleontologist's nightmare. You see those peaks over there? That was a volcano, and so was that, and that."

Vinny looked. She had no idea how far away the mountains were, but there was snow on the cone-shaped summits, white, magical, where the blue range rose to meet the immense and even bluer sky. She'd have known those were volcanoes without his telling her.

"Have you done plate tectonics yet?" he said.

"Last term."

"Well, we're right at the point where the plate carrying Asia moves against the one carrying Africa. In one way this is terrific, because there've been a whole series of eruptions, which have laid down layers of volcanic ash, which in theory you can date by scientific methods. But at the same time the ground has been churned around and shoved to and fro and turned upside down, even, so you get a series of strata in one place, and half a mile away they're the other way up, or whole sections are missing. Joe brought a geologist, but she took one look at the place and told him that any dates she came up with would be give or take a million years each way, and being Joe he tried to teach her her own business, so she said she was sick and pulled out. That was one thing. Then again, being Joe he's quarreled with so many people that he couldn't get any responsible organization to fund him, so we're funded by people no one takes seriously, and that in turn means that a lot of the team are beginners or second-raters. Not that Joe minds. Second-raters are easier to impress. And he hasn't got anyone to run the camp properly and can't be bothered himself, so I'm having to spend half my time sorting things out for him . . . Oh, God. I'm sorry."

He sounded ashamed of himself. It had all come bursting out of him, unstoppable, like an eruption from one of the volcanoes he'd pointed out. He was a bottler-up, Vinny guessed. That was what the silences were about, perhaps, anger going around and around inside his head while he tried to tame it, master it. He really needed someone he didn't mind bursting out to. Mom wouldn't have been any use—she'd have been full of suggestions, 1,001 Things to Do, Colin called it. That wasn't what Dad needed.

"It's all right," she said. "It's much easier for me, knowing. I hope there's someone there you like a bit."

He laughed.

"Oh yes, of course. Several of them. In fact . . . Well, as I said, you'll see."

Then

The child who had trapped the shark had no name, nor did the others. As a baby she'd known her mother and had made sucking movements when she came near, and she still sometimes did this, a lip sound, *Ma-ma,* but it was more an affectionate greeting than a name. Later she'd begun to recognize the others, her mother's sister first, then other close family, then playmates, all as separate people who mattered in different ways to her. By the time of the shark hunt she knew every member of the tribe, and they knew her, but without names.

(I must use names to tell their story. We are looking into our furthest possible past, which is like looking at a group of people far off across a flat, hot plain. The rising air wavers and changes. Light bends as if it were passing through invisible lenses. The people seem to dwindle, stretch, vanish, stand clear for a moment, and distort again. We are looking through lenses of time, right at the edge of imagination's eyesight. To give the tribe names distorts them, but it's the best I can do from where we're standing. It's said that before Eve there was Lilith, but we are going back far beyond the imaginary Lilith. I shall call the child Li.

The same with her thoughts. We have to imagine them in words, but the tribe were only about halfway toward words. Their ancestors had been apes, who had used calls for alarm and anger and so on, but had mainly communicated by gestures, grimaces, smells, and touch. Then the sea had risen and those ancestors had been cut off on a large offshore island. At the same time Africa had grown hotter and drier, and the forest cover where the ancestors had lived and fed had dried out and almost vanished, so they'd started to forage for the rich pickings along the shore, taking more and more to the water, changing in many ways. Among these were their calls. Smell was no use to them in water, gestures difficult. Except in a dead, flat sea a swimmer can see only a few yards, but a call will still be heard far off.

So the tribe had plenty of calls—*Come help, Shark!, Big wave!, Follow me, Good food this way, Praise, Triumph, Have mercy,* and so on. And when they came out of their caves in the morning, or rose on one of their roosting ledges to let the rising sun warm their night-chilled bodies, they sang. These were all calls, not words, not sentences. But how can we imagine Li's thoughts without using words? We are looking through the time lens again, distorting what was, then, into something we seem to see, now. It's the best we can do.)

The wind had shifted and the tribe had moved on down the coastline to where an immense sea marsh blocked their way. Once it had been the channel between their island and the shore, but the land had risen and the island was ceasing to be an island. They didn't like the marsh. They were creatures of the coast, of clean rocks and beaches.

Immediately north of the marsh lay a stretch of pure, fine sand where, for a few days at each full moon as the tides came higher, the shallows swarmed with millions upon millions of almost invisible transparent shrimp. The tribe caught them by lacing their cupped hands together with the fingertips just touching the webbing between the lower knuckles of the other hand. When they lifted their hands and let the water drain away a few shrimp might be left wriggling in the trap.

It was slow feeding, but Li was clever at it and had eaten her fill while most of the others were still busy. She felt a need to be alone, out of the crowded shallows. If she swam further from the shore the shark watchers would summon her back. The beach itself was roasting hot, so she climbed the low dunes behind it, looking for shade. In front of her the mountain chain that had formed the island rose steep and barren, but between the shore and the first rocks lay a strip of plain which itself had been beach and shallows until this end of the island had tilted upward. Now it was hard earth, mottled with tussocks of coarse grass, and here and there a tree. One stood, or rather leaned, not far off, so after a wary look around she made for it.

(Suppose for a moment that the time lens lets us see her undistorted, what does she look like, this single, night-black figure crossing the glaring flat? She walks erect, but is still not quite a meter tall. Her body is hairless but her head has a glossy black mane falling over her shoulders. She is plump, roly-poly, from the layer of insulating fat beneath her skin. Her feet are like ours, but webbed between the toes, and her long fingers have webs to the first knuckle. Her head is the shock, tiny to our eyes, with a face more monkey than human. What room can there be in that cramped skull for thoughts, imaginations, questions, wonders, for all that makes us human? Can this be where we came from?)

From the shade of the tree Li studied the plain. She felt excited but tense. She had never been so far from the tribe alone. She didn't know what there was to be afraid of—there could be no sharks out here and she'd never seen a leopard, but the instinct was still there, deep inside. Another instinct made her climb into the crotch of the tree, and on up until she was well above ground level. Now she relaxed a little.

The tree had been flat-topped once, but an earthquake had tilted it so that on one side its branches touched the ground and on the other they lifted enough for her to see out beneath them. She stared, amazed, at the distance. Before her lay the marsh. From the shore it had seemed endless, but now beyond it she saw a wavering line of blue, rising to peaks from two of which thin trails of smoke drifted skyward. She recognized them because there was another such peak at the center of the island. Sometimes it flamed, sometimes it rumbled or groaned, but mostly it merely smoked, peaceful and harmless.

Li stared entranced at the view. The fifty miles or so of island shore which was the tribe's territory was all she had ever known, all the world there was. Now, over there beyond the marshes, she saw another world, immense.

Cramp broke the trance, making her shift her position. Then a flick of movement caught her eye, speed followed by stillness, like a minnow in a pool. It had happened where the spread twigs of the tree swept down to the earth. Inquisitive, she climbed down and crept across to see.

The spider was crouched over its prey, bouncing gently on its springy legs. Spiders were no good to eat. The bug it had caught might have been, but Li wasn't hungry. She

wanted to see what the spider would do. She crouched and
watched while the spider dragged the bug clear of the
insect-size track along which it had been scuttling. It
climbed into the twigs above the track and rapidly wove a
coarse, loose web, then returned to earth and stretched a
couple of threads across the path. It moved into the shadows and waited. So did Li.

Nothing happened. Her absorption dwindled. She became aware of the dry, alien plain around her, and her
distance from the tribe. Every insect click, every faint rus-
tle, might be a danger sound. She must go back. But first
she needed to know what the spider was up to. There was
no reason for the need, no purpose or use in knowing. It
was the mere knowledge that mattered.

Moving as carefully as if she'd been stalking a minnow,
she pulled a grass stem from a tussock and, starting some
distance from the web, trailed the seed head along the
path. It moved jerkily, like a crawling bug. As it touched
the threads the web tumbled from above, tangling loosely
around it, and the spider had leapt and was crouching over
it to inspect its prey. Li couldn't see what had triggered the
web to fall.

She watched the spider strip the remains of web from
the seed head and eat them. The stem was too heavy for it
to draw the seed head clear of the path, so it chose a new
place, built another web trap and waited. Li peered closely,
trying to see how the web was made, but it was too
complicated for her. The sense of danger returned, overwhelming her longing for knowledge, so she gave up and
returned to the beach.

The tide was ebbing and there were no more shrimp, so
the tribe were resting in the shallows. Li chose a place a
little apart, deep enough for her to float upright, ducking
her head now and then to rewet her thatch of hair against

the fierce sun. She could have dozed like that, as the others were doing, but the excitement of thought kept her awake. There were two pictures in her mind, the minnow in the pool and the web dropping from the twigs. Northward there were rock pools with minnows in them. A yellow one was especially delicious, but almost impossible to catch. But if she could make a web . . . How . . . ? With what . . . ?

Toward evening she crossed the dunes again and collected the longest grass stems she could find. Returning to the beach she scooped away the burning surface, making a cooler hollow where she could sit and work at the problem, stopping only when it was too dark to see. She got nowhere. The stems were brittle and wouldn't stay together, her fingers didn't understand what she wanted them to do, but she remained absorbed. The failures themselves were knowledge, feeding her need.

Here the tribe slept in scooped nests in the sand, some always wakeful in case of danger. At the midnight tide they woke and shrimped through the shallows under the white full moon as their ancestors had done for thousands of generations, on this beach, at this tide. They didn't need memories or knowledge to wake at the proper time. The tide was in their blood and called to them. The shrimp were easier to catch at night because they were phosphorescent, moving in drifting sheets of light above the rippled sand. This was how it always had been. It could not change.

Climbing the dunes next morning for fresh grass stems, Li noticed a fragment of netlike orange stuff protruding from the wind-blown sand. She pulled it free and found that it was no larger than the webbing between two of her fingers. It was in fact gourd fiber, left after the flesh of the gourd had rotted away, and then blown onto the dunes. Li tested it and found how delicate it was, and far too small in any case, so she went on and collected her grass stems. In the night the notion had come to her that they were brittle because they were dry, and if she wetted them she might have more luck. This helped a little, but soon the sun became too hot for further work on shore, and in the water the grass stems floated about uncontrollably, so she gave up.

Then she remembered that she had sometimes seen bigger pieces of gourd fiber, so she went and searched the dunes till she found one about as large as her spread hand. At the noon tide she tried it out. She was still thinking of minnows. She hadn't intended to use it to catch shrimp—she could do that with her hands—and only wanted to see how the mesh worked, but at her first trawl she found several transparent bodies wriggling on the net. Delicately she picked them out, calling *Come and see* to Ma-ma.

The fragile mesh soon tore, so she supported it with both hands, cupping them in the usual way but with more space between the fingers so that the water drained quickly away, leaving the shrimp trapped. As the swarms increased she was catching twenty or thirty at a time, and Ma-ma picked them off and fed both of them. The females and young used to start the shrimping, with the males joining in only when there were enough for them to catch with their clumsier fingers, so at first Li was able to keep her invention to herself while Ma-ma shooed the others away. Then the males arrived.

Since the shark hunt Li's uncle Presh had without an actual fight challenged and outfaced old Mirn and become the undisputed leader of the tribe. It was in his interest to investigate any commotion among the lesser members, and since Li's invention was causing a stir of interest he waded over to see what was happening. Humbly she offered him a meshful of shrimp which he picked greedily off, ruining the mesh as he did so.

Without resentment she returned to shrimping with her bare hands, and then rested in the water, thinking not about webs or nets but reliving the wonder of seeing that far, blue other world across the marshes.

Now:
Sunday Evening

Dr. Joe Hamiska was tall and scrawny, with a dark red-brown beard flecked with gray. He dressed a bit like someone in an old film about African explorers, with leather walking boots and baggy shorts and a white cotton shirt open at the neck to show a few gray hairs on his tanned chest.

He said, "Hi, there," to Vinny, and smiled; but before Dad could introduce her to anyone else he said, "We've got problems, Sam. The Craig people have switched their dates. They're coming Thursday."

"I don't see it makes much difference," said Dad.

"Oh, but it does, Sam, it does. Come and look at this."

He took Dad over to a trestle table under an awning and gave him a sheet of paper but kept on talking so that he couldn't read it. From what Dad had said in the truck Vinny guessed that this was to show her and everyone else that working for Dr. Hamiska was much more important than having your daughter visit you.

She didn't mind. She was floating in a pool of

happiness because she was here at last. She'd made it, against all the odds, since that Christmas twenty months ago. Tom had just learned to read so Mom had sent him to get the presents from the Christmas tree and sort them into piles in the living room while the rest of them cleared up breakfast. They'd come in and found that he'd put four piles together by the sofa and one, Vinny's, separately by the armchair. Of course he hadn't meant anything, not consciously, but there'd been a meaning all the same, obvious as a jeer. Colin had laughed and muddled the piles up and told everyone to find their own and made a fuss of Vinny, but while she was picking the Scotch tape off her first present and folding the paper away before looking to see what Gran had sent her, she was thinking, *I want my own dad.* After lunch she'd written a long thank-you letter for his check, not asking for anything, not complaining, but with questions in it which he'd have to answer. So her campaign had started, and now here she was.

She looked around. Only twenty minutes before it had been daylight and they'd been driving through barren, hummocky ground which Dad had called badlands. Then they'd climbed to the camp among a few sparse trees on the first slope of hills, and already it was almost dark. The plain below had changed color as she'd watched, from brown and gray and orange to nearly black. She felt she was seeing the shadow of the world rise up as the sun set behind her and the eastern stars emerged. The air was still, and thick, and hot.

The camp was huts, tents, and larger awnings. Butane lamps had been lit. Close by Vinny a woman working at a trestle table pushed her spectacles onto her forehead with a weary gesture and looked up.

"Hi," she said. "You're Vinny. I'm May Anna. I guess you're tired after the trip."

"Dad made me a nest in the back of the truck after lunch and I slept till we were almost here. Can I see what you're doing?"

May Anna was about thirty-five, Vinny guessed, obviously American, thin, with lanky pale hair in a ponytail. She wore a T-shirt and denim shorts. The lenses of her spectacles were the size of saucers.

"Sure," she said. "You like jigsaws?"

"Sometimes."

"Have a go at this one."

On the table were what looked like flakes of stone arranged in rows on two trays. Most of them were smaller than a penny. Between the trays was a rounded blob of Plasticine, onto which a few flakes had been fitted together to form two irregular patches, each about half the size of Vinny's palm.

"Is it someone's skull?" she said.

"Correct. A fellow called *Homo habilis,* maybe. Maybe not. Looks like we've got about half a cranium, if we can fit it together. This bit here."

May Anna ran her fingers spiderlike over the back of her head.

"How old is it?" said Vinny.

"If he's *habilis,* could be two million, two and a half million years."

"Wow!"

From the books Dad had told her to read Vinny knew that *habilis* meant something that had been about halfway human, a bit like an upright-walking baboon with a much bigger brain. There'd been other somethings with other names, and no one agreed which of them had really been the ancestor of modern humans. No one seemed to agree about anything, much. They'd find a bit of jaw or a kneebone and say it was really important and different from what anyone else had found and proved all the others were wrong and there'd be a colossal argument until someone found something else. Then they'd all gang up against the newcomer.

"I'm used to it," said May Anna. "But I still wake up nights and think about all those years and my skin crawls. Know what I mean?"

Vinny peered at the flakes of fossil each in its numbered square. The empty squares showed where the ones which May Anna had fitted into place came from.

"It's worse than a jigsaw," she said. "You haven't got a picture."

"We have, though," said May Anna. "Look."

She held one of the larger chips slantwise to the lamplight.

"See those wrinkles?" she said. "Know what they are? They're the pattern on the surface of the brain beneath."

"I can't see anything . . . Oh, yes . . . No . . ."

May Anna picked up another flake and held it against the first, edge on.

"Your eyes have to learn to see, know what I mean?" she said. "But look here—they just don't belong. They don't . . . Hey! Look at this! They do!"

Laughing, she turned one chip through ninety degrees and put the two edges together. They fitted as if they'd only just been snapped apart. They overlapped, leaving a triangular space each side of the join. May Anna, still crowing, turned them over and pressed them onto the Plasticine mold, tilting her head this way and that to study them.

"Somedays you don't get a single darned fit," she said. "Now a pointy bit—I've seen it, I know I've seen it! There . . . And look! Hey! Sam! Come see what we've got here!"

She'd called to Dad, but it was Dr. Hamiska who reached the table first. Then everyone was crowding around to watch her fit the three new pieces against one of the existing patches, and then chip by chip ease the other patch loose and join it on with the new pieces bridging the gap. Everyone started talking together.

"I guess I've got it wrongly oriented," said May Anna, twisting her hand above the surface to show which way she thought the skull now went.

"It's too small," said someone. "It can't be *habilis*."

"Who said it was?" said someone else.

"It's certainly too small," said Dr. Hamiska. "A good two hundred cc too small, I think. You're going to have to take that out of your base mold, May Anna."

"I was just quitting and I picked out a couple of pieces to show Vinny, and what do you know? They fitted. I wasn't even trying."

"Then you've brought us luck, Vinny," said Dr. Hamiska. "You must keep it up."

"If it's smaller than *habilis,* then it's older than *habilis,*" said someone.

"Exactly," said Dr. Hamiska. "A million years at least. Two million. And look here . . ."

He ran a stubby forefinger over the surface of the patch, following some kind of line Vinny couldn't see.

"We must have something a layman can understand," he said. "And by Thursday."

It wasn't just a wish or a hope, it was an order. An order to the universe. He was peering and poking among the fragments as if he could will them into showing him how they fitted. Dad's letters had made him sound a tiresome old geezer, but now, meeting him, Vinny found him more alarming than irritating. His personality was like some kind of sci-fi force-field which he could beam out of

himself when he wanted, and if you came within range, it
made you his slave. The fossils, though, were immune to
the force-field and gave up none of their secrets, so after a
minute he switched it off, straightened, and smiled.

"Well done, Vinny. I can see you're going to be useful."

"I didn't do anything."

"You brought us luck. I take luck very seriously. I'm
sorry I couldn't let Sam go with you on safari, but he's the
best there is and I can't do without him."

"I'd much rather come here. This is really interesting."

"We'll make a paleontologist of you yet. Well, thanks,
Sam. And well done, May Anna—that's going to be a
great help with the Craig people. If only we could get a
line on the dating—let's have another look at your pig
data, Fred . . ."

He rushed off to one of the awnings. A thin man did a
Woody Allen shrug and followed him. The others hung
around studying the jigsaw and searching the trays for further fits until May Anna shooed them away before they
could muddle her arrangements. Dad stayed. He was the
only one who hadn't joined in the chatter around the
skull.

"What do you think, Sam?" said May Anna.

"I think maybe. Just don't let him rush you or you'll be
forcing the evidence. It's quite unnecessary, this hoo-ha
about Thursday."

"You don't have to raise the money, Sam. More important right now, I could do with a drink."

"So could I. What about you, Vinny. Coke?"

"Anything."

He left and May Anna packed up, covering the trays
with weighted plastic sheets and putting an upturned
bucket over the precious skull.

"Who are the Craig people?" said Vinny.

"Well now, there was this kid from Colorado called Oscar Craig who used to go wandering up into the hills looking for dinosaur fossils. This would be around eighteen ninety-something, I guess. Then his dad ran out on the family and his ma moved to Denver where he went to college. He was a bright kid, learned chemistry, was hired by a company, developed a depilatory, from that moved into cosmetics, and before he was forty he was running his own business. By the time he died he was one of the richest men in America. He'd married but there were no kids. What he'd done with his money was collect art—Impressionists and older stuff—but I guess that was because it was kind of expected of him, you know? What he really liked was still fossils. He spent a lot of money trying to prove that people came to America long before the textbooks said they did. When he died he set up the Craig Museum back in Denver, mainly for his art collection, but he put it into his will that it's got to have a paleontology department too. When Joe was trying to raise funds to get us out here, the Craig people were the only ones he could get interested. Nobody in the field takes them that seriously, you see, but Joe told them he'd really put them on the map, bring them back fossils of Adam and Eve almost, so that all the other fossil freaks would have to sit up and take notice. Now the people from Craig are coming out to see what he's got for their money, and all he'll have to show them is this little fellow here."

She tapped the upturned bucket and laughed. Dad came back with the drinks, passed one casually to May Anna and gave Vinny hers a bit more formally. He hadn't asked May Anna what sort she wanted either. And earlier he'd twice started to tell Vinny about something or someone special on this expedition, and then stopped himself and said she'd see. She didn't say anything now, but sipped her Coke. It was just what she wanted.

"How did you get it cold?" she said. "Have you got a fridge?"

"Any fool can be uncomfortable in camp," said Dad.

"And any camp with Sam in it is as good as a Hilton," said May Anna. "It's a big deal when we run out of canned crabmeat. He's down in the books as our taphonomist, but that's just an excuse. We have him to run the camp."

"Too true to be funny," said Dad. "Let's go and unpack your stuff and I'll show you the layout. Then it should be supper time."

Supper was beef curry and rice with fresh vegetables and fruit which Dad had bought at a market near the airport last evening. They ate at trestle tables. Dr. Hamiska made a fuss of introducing Vinny all around, too many names to remember. Vinny sat with Dad and May Anna and Fred, Dr. Wessler, the one who knew about pigs. The talk was all about the skull, and how much Plasticine May Anna ought to take out to give it the right-sized brain. Vinny couldn't understand the detail but she could hear their excitement, though Dad was trying to be cautious and Dr. Wessler kept telling May Anna—only half as a joke and half, Vinny guessed, because he was the kind of person who actually gets a kick out of things going wrong—that she'd got bits of baboon skull muddled up with her hominid fragments. Vinny was dropping with sleep by the time the meal ended, but she couldn't go to bed because Dad had said she mustn't go to the latrines alone in the dark, in case of leopards or something.

At last May Anna said, "Looks like you'd better take Vinny to bed, Sam," and he remembered he'd got a daughter.

On their way back from the latrines he said, "I'm sure I

needn't tell you, but just in case. What I was saying about Joe, in the truck after lunch—you won't say anything about that to anyone, will you?"

"No, of course not . . . What about May Anna?"

"Oh, she's all right."

"I think she's lovely."

"I'm glad you like her."

Then

Li woke in the night. There were no caves at this other bay, but good roosting ledges where the tribe could huddle for warmth. She turned on her back and watched the stars, at first in a thoughtless, dreamy wonder, but then, as they vanished one by one behind the black lip of the cliff above, in wakeful amazement. They were moving, in just the same way the sun moved through the sky by day. The whole vast heavens moved all together, like the march of rollers toward the shore. She gazed, rapt, waiting for each prick of light to blank out, until she heard Ma-ma mutter a call in her sleep: *Careful, little one.*

Ma-ma must be dreaming. At once Li fell into a new wonder that someone could dream, as she herself dreamed, inside her own head as she slept, seeing and knowing things that nobody else would ever see or know. Ma-ma, who lay so close, was utterly other. Utterly not-Li. All of them, all the tribe. Other. Before the last rains a stranger had joined the tribe, a female with a dying baby. Where had she come from? Somewhere beyond the tribe's

territory, which ended at a crocodile-infested river to the
north. How had she come? Why? There were no answers.
These things were the stranger's, as other as Ma-ma's
dreams.

The stranger had hung around on the fringes of the
tribe for a few days and then they'd accepted her, but her
baby had died. Where had it gone? Not the body—the
stranger had carried that back into the dunes and left it—
but the little sick person who'd looked out of the weary
eyes? That too was other, never-to-be-known, like
dreams. The stranger seemed to have forgotten her baby
and her grief, but Li hadn't.

Li didn't sleep again. She watched the stars fade and
vanish, and before the rest of the tribe began to stir,
climbed down and made her way out to the rock spit that
half enclosed the bay. From here she could see the central
volcano of the island already bright with the rising sun, but
her mind didn't take it in except as part of the whole
strange, marvelous world, whose hugeness and otherness
she was learning to recognize. At first she was shuddering
with cold, then the sun rose, warming her through, tin-
gling her skin with animal pleasures, but she barely noticed
either the cold or the comfort. She felt she was close to
something enormous, some knowledge—not a piece of
knowledge, like how to bash a mussel open on a rock or
the way the stars moved—but a whole knowledge. The
knowledge had the shape of a question. It seemed to fill
her world like the light of the rising sun, to send tremors of
its presence through her like the warming sun rays. Other
questions, the ones about using and seeing, she was outside
of. She could study them and think and find their answers.
This one she was inside of, part of. In fact she was herself
the question. To answer it she would need to become
somehow other, as other as Ma-ma's dreams or the

stranger's lost baby. Perhaps she would need to go where the baby had gone.

Ma-ma rose with a slither and slop beside the rocks and broke in on Li's trance by making disapproval clicks and sluicing water over her, the way mothers did until their children were old enough to know that as the sun rose they had to stay in the water or in shadow, or at least keep their bodies wet through the heat of the day. The skins of the tribe were a very dark purply brown and almost as thick as pigskin, but an hour in the unveiled noon sun could still make them burn.

In fact it was not yet that hot, but Ma-ma was fussing, partly because she was heavily pregnant and partly because she was puzzled by Li's behavior. The others took it for granted, in the same way that they took for granted Bola's passion for scooping holes in the sand for no purpose at all. They didn't consider that Li's lonely trances or her rapt experiments in any way affected them, though some of them were already becoming expert with the minnow nets she'd invented.

On the northward journey from the shrimping beach Li had noticed a mat of gourd vine draped down a cliff. It was a common plant of that coast, but the tribe ignored it because the gourds were inedible, but now Li had made the connection with the fragments she'd used for shrimp-ing, and had found that fallen gourds in the right state of decay contained intact and stronger nets which could be washed free of the pulp and then used to trap small prey. Carefully treated such a net might last a whole day.

Li herself was not satisfied with the discovery. She'd seen the spider *make* its trap. She wanted to make some-thing too, and experimented with grass stems, with sea-weed fronds, with vine strands, with the long, coarse reeds that grew by the northern river. Most of her trials ended in failure. The materials were so weak and hard to fasten, her fingers so clumsy. It took her three journeys to the shrimping beach and back before she achieved her first knot. But failure didn't matter. The real excitement lay in thinking. Her days were electric with thought. It was better than food, better than warmth, better than sleep. At dusk she would lie down and fight off sleep so that she could think a little longer, and wake with a rush of joy that she could begin again.

But Ma-ma felt that children should be like other children. There'd been a gap in her pregnancies, and Li was still the most important person in her life. Li understood this and was glad of it, so now she slid down into the water and hugged and kissed her as they dipped below the surface. Still holding each other, they kicked gently away from the rocks, with the ripple-patterned sunlight wavering across their bodies. They kissed again as they rose for breath, and then Ma-ma swam off to look for food.

Li should have gone too. Her stomach was empty, but she wanted to return to the trance of thought. A gang of young came foaming out to the rock spit to play the running game, crying to her to join in. They lined up a pace apart in the water with only their heads above the surface, while the runner climbed ashore and then tried to run out along the line, using the heads as stepping-stones. Just as the foot came down the swimmer kicked up to take the weight, and if they all timed it right the runner reached the end of the line and dived triumphantly into deep water, then joined the line while the next runner climbed out.

This was a good place for the game, but Li watched only a turn or two before swimming off to the other side of the spit to drift and think. Here she was in open sea, so she fell into the rhythm of shark watch, with her head below the surface, ready for any large, shadowy movement in the clear water. She kept one hand on a jag of rock and now and then eased herself up for a fresh lungful, then sank again. She did this automatically, without effort, but perhaps it was a slight distraction, or perhaps watching the game had broken the thread, or perhaps the intensity of thought itself had exhausted it, but whatever the cause Li found she couldn't bring back the rapt, overwhelming wonder of being she had felt as she'd sat on the rocks while the sun rose.

All that came to her was fragments, memories of how it had felt, like reflections in a pool disturbed by a splash. Now she became aware of her hunger, and was about to swim off and forage when she saw a movement in the water, not a single shape but a small shoal of fish, hurtling toward her. Something was hunting them. She clutched the rock, ready to leap to safety. To the fish Li's body must have seemed part of the dark rock, along which they swerved aside, their bodies almost brushing against her. Catching fish in open sea was a matter of luck, but she timed her strike right, grabbed one, gripped it in her teeth, and shot herself out onto the rock.

She shook the wet hair from her eyes with the fish still threshing in her mouth. Immediately below her a dolphin surged past, its back arching out of the calm sea. She had never seen one so close.

Li knew about dolphins. Once the tribe had found a stranded one, dead and decaying, and had feasted on it and then been ill. They saw several hunting together, sometimes. Though dolphins came, like sharks, from the mysterious, vast outer sea, they weren't dangerous to people.

The fish convulsed as she bit out a chunk of back muscle and started to chew, delighted with not having to waste time foraging. Perhaps she might go and join the game— they sounded as if they were having fun . . . She bit and chewed again, wondering at herself. Why wasn't that kind of fun so important to her now? Why had she changed since the shark hunt? She'd been perfectly happy before . . .

She had her right knee drawn up under her chin but her left leg dangled toward the water. Something nudged it. One of her friends must have swum around under the surface to tease her. She pretended not to notice, but at the next nudge glanced disdainfully down. It was the dolphin.

It hung, poised in the water, its blunt nose poking at her ankle. She snatched her leg away. The dolphin half followed, sank, nosed up again. Li bit another chunk from the fish and then leaned over the water, dangling it teasingly by its tail. Effortlessly the dolphin rose and took the fish from her hand, with its gleaming pale underside showing clear before, with barely a splash, it flipped over and down.

They were strong signals in the tribe, the giving and taking of food. They meant friendship, alliance, trust. Without hesitation Li dived into the sea and waited, tense but thrilled. The dolphin was several times her size. If it had been a shark it could have killed her outright, but it drifted slowly toward her and past, brushing its long, smooth flank against her chest. She watched it turn and come back. This time as it passed she slid her arm around its body and laid her own body trailing against its flank as it swam. It accepted her for a little, but then seemed to become alarmed and sprang violently forward. Alarmed herself she let go and rose for breath, and seeing that she was now well away from the rocks paddled quickly back, dipped below, and waited again.

She thought it had gone, but when she had risen for several more breaths she saw a vague shape moving at the limits of her underwater vision. She swam a little out from the rocks and watched it zigzag warily in till it stopped, just out of reach. They faced each other, poised in the water, until she was forced to surface for breath.

Again they faced each other and again she was forced to surface, but this time it rose too and snorted a cloudy spout from the hole in the top of its head, its gasp echoing hers. Now it let her edge closer, until she could reach out and carefully touch its snout. As she stroked its forehead it came in and past her, brushing against her side as before, turning and coming back. This time when she reached her arm around it she was careful to clasp it only loosely, and it seemed to decide to let her stay there until she had to let go and rise for breath. It was waiting for her when she dived.

They swam, played, danced together in the sunlit ocean and her sense of wonder came back, but changed. This was not a thinking wonder, but a wonder like the sunlight, pure, itself and nothing else. Or it was as if she and the dolphin were themselves thoughts in the delighting mind of the sea, moving with the same exhilaration as the thoughts that moved through her mind, telling her that she was in the presence of, part of, an immense mystery. The dolphin was far more other than Ma-ma's dreams, or the stranger's lost baby, but it and Li shared the moment and the mystery in the rippling golden-green water.

So it was a timeless while before she saw, rising for breath, how far their game had taken them from the shore. The dolphin rose beside her as if to ask what kept her so long out in the barren air, and she put an arm around it and gestured with her other arm toward the land, confident that it would understand what she wanted. Now she needed to clasp it close as it used its full power to surge through the water, arching clear and plunging under, while she gasped and laughed with the excitement of the ride. For a few moments she knew what it was like to be a dolphin, to share in the life of the open ocean.

Kerif, on shark watch, saw them coming without understanding what he was seeing. At his shout of *Shark!* the dolphin swerved aside, so Li let go and swam on alone. Reaching Kerif, she gave him the respectful triple hoot which a she-child used on meeting an adult male, but he stared at her with his mouth hanging open and forgot to answer.

Now:
Monday Morning

Vinny woke in the dark and using the flashlight Dad had lent her found it was half-past five. She desperately needed a pee, but she knew she mustn't go till it was light. At home the bathroom was right next door to her own room, and she could find her way there with her eyes shut, almost without waking up. Here it was way down the hill, and there might be leopards, and she had to wait till it was light. Homesickness had suddenly ambushed her. It was stupid. She was thrilled to be here, but why couldn't they have a bathroom next door?

Dad was breathing snortily on the other side of the room, which was half of a neat round hut with a grass roof. She had a mosquito net over her bed, but something had bitten her left arm all the same. It was all right—once Mom had accepted that Vinny was really going to Africa, she'd taken charge and made sure she had all the right injections and took all the right pills. She'd even gone up to London and got special stuff from the British Airways shop in Regent Street. She'd been a real help, not just bossy. Now, lying in the dark, feeling homesick, Vinny was conscious that she hadn't been quite fair when she'd talked to Dad about Mom yesterday. She hadn't wanted to put him off. But Mom wasn't just your average decent parent, she was A1 most of the time, brimming with interest and love and energy. Fun. Of course she went over the top sometimes, but it was worth it, especially with Colin around to laugh her out of her wilder ideas. Vinny guessed that Dad wouldn't have known how to do that. He'd have just closed down, gone silent, and Mom would have got wilder and wilder to compensate. Perhaps that had been what went wrong.

As soon as it was light she slid out of the narrow bed, tapped out her slippers in case scorpions had decided they'd make a cozy lair (Dad had warned her about that), wrapped her parka around her and crept out. Day came as fast as it had gone. On the way up the path from the latrines she found that Africa had its own smell, which the dawn dew brought out, faint and sharp, like cold wet iron, plus an animal smell—not death or dung or urine because the sun dried things out before they could rot, but the living hide. She felt as if the whole continent might be a single sleeping animal, with its own special odor. You didn't get that on TV.

Not wanting to wake Dad—he'd seemed really tired last night, with the long drive, or perhaps with his own anger —she drifted around the camp, exploring. One of the awnings covered rows of fossils, laid out with numbered cards in places. She decided they must all be bits of jaw, or single teeth. The numbers read 1.6, 1.8, 2.0, and so on up to 4.8. These must be Dr. Wessler's pigs, she thought, and the numbers would be millions of years. More than half the fossils seemed to be somewhere around the four-million-year mark. All those pigs! There must have been thousands and thousands of them, rootling and snuffling. What did pigs like? Boggy sorts of places, reeds, marshes, wallows. Or had pigs been different then? If we'd evolved out of pigs instead of monkeys, what would we be like? Try that on Dad.

The camp began to stir. Someone was cooking. An African came in under the awning. She remembered his face from last night, long and narrow with rather protruding teeth, but not his name. He smiled and answered when she said "Good morning," then went to a particular place in the lines of fossils, picked one of them up, and took it out into the open, where he stood studying it, turning it this way and that. Beyond him Vinny saw Dad at the door of the hut, gazing blearily out as if he was looking for her. She ran across.

"You're an early bird," he said. "Sleep well?"

"Fine, thanks. Do dads get kissed good-morning in our family?"

"No harm in trying."

He seemed in a much better humor than yesterday. He fetched a bowl of warm water so that she could wash and dress while he went down to the latrines, and then another bowl for himself.

"Hang on a mo. I'm just doing my laces."

"No hurry."

By the time Vinny looked up he had stripped off his pajama top and was brushing his teeth. He had the most incredibly hairy chest. It was difficult not to stare. Funny that Mom, who sometimes used to tell anyone listening about things to do with Dad that had niggled her, had never mentioned it. He saw her looking, and with his toothbrush sticking sideways out of his mouth stretched and beat his chest like a gorilla. She laughed.

"That reminds me," she said. "This book I read—it wasn't one of the ones you said, but it was on the same shelf. It said the reason we don't have fur like chimps and gorillas . . ."

"Some of us don't," he mumbled, still brushing.

". . . is that we're really half sea-animals."

He rinsed his mouth out and spat as if the toothpaste had suddenly tasted wrong.

"It was really interesting, Dad. The sea rose and there must have been an island which got cut off with a few apes on it, and they had to get most of their food out of the sea, so they learned to walk on their hind legs and they lost their fur and used stones to crack shells open, oh, and all sorts of other things. Language. And did you know if you put your face underwater, your heart slows down to help you hold your breath? And we've got fat under our skins and our tears are salty . . . Why didn't any of the other books mention all that? I thought they were mean."

"She's not respectable."

"But she's interesting, Dad. I've got her name in my diary. Hold on. What do you mean, respectable? And she made me laugh. Not a lot of laughs in the other books. Here—Elaine Morgan. Have you read it?"

"As a matter of fact, no."

"Darn. There's a lot of things I wanted to ask you about it. I mean, fur. You know before we're born we've got fur on our bodies for a bit? She says that with us it's sort of streamlined, for swimming, but it isn't with chimps and gorillas. Is that right?"

"I wouldn't know. I'm only a taphonomist."

"That's what I mean. You all know your own bits, and you're so absolutely sure they're the most important . . . I'm sorry . . . But it was interesting."

She had stopped because she had sensed a change in him, a closing down. She'd thought she'd been just teasing, but now she realized she'd gone too far in some way

she didn't understand. But at the same time she sensed he
hadn't wanted it to happen. She could see the disappoint-
ment in his eyes.

"I'm sorry," she said again. "You'll have to tell me."

He sighed, made an effort, and managed to shake himself out of the mood.

"Just remember you're your mother's daughter," he
said. "You can tell me about the fur, if you insist."

"All right. Stand still. Do you mind?"

He made a clown face as he spread his arms and allowed
her to run her fingers through the mat of hair on his chest,
trying to feel for the flow lines.

"I don't know," she said. "I need a chimp to compare
you with."

"The nearest chimp is several hundred miles away. May
I put my shirt on?"

"All right. Do you honestly think it's nonsense?"

"I think there isn't any serious evidence for it. I think in
fact there is very little serious evidence for *any* theories of
early hominid evolution."

"But we aren't chimps, Dad. *Something* happened. We're
different."

"That's the trouble. Now clear out, will you, while I
finish dressing."

The camp was busier now, with people going to and fro,
getting ready for the day. The man who'd taken the fossil
from the awning was sitting at one of the tables, sketching
it. Vinny moved closer to watch. He was using a very hard
pencil, so that the lines he made were almost invisible.
Each movement he made was slow, firm, exact. Already
the nobbly, shapeless lump on the table seemed to have
become clear and ordered on the pad.

After a few minutes he put his pencil down to stretch

and yawn. He was clearly surprised to see Vinny standing so close.

"That's beautiful," she said. "I'm afraid I've forgotten your name."

"Thank you. I'm Nikki Mako. Now you're going to say why don't I just take a photograph?"

"But you can see a lot more in a drawing."

"You're right. Know what? I don't know nothing about fossils. I'm at college studying commercial art when the Minister tells our Principal he better find some fellows to come on Joe's expedition, right?"

"Why did they choose you?"

" 'Cause I get this prize last year. They send us along to the museum, tell us go and draw something for the competition, so I draw this big old dinosaur and I win the prize, you know?"

He laughed at the joke. His eyes were lively with the absurdity. Despite being narrow set they didn't make him look mean, any more than his prominent teeth made him look ugly. They were right for him.

"Well, they're lucky to get someone who can draw like you," said Vinny.

He shook his head and studied the half-finished picture.

"No use for them. They take photographs, casts, you know. This is for me. My way of seeing a thing. Learning it, you know. Fred Wessler, he can tell you all about this fossil 'cause he's seen don't know how many hundred fossil, all the same sort, looked at them, felt them in his hands. That's his way. This is my way. When I draw something, I look at it like it was the only damn thing in the world, only thing I'm ever going to be let see again. Know what I mean?"

"I'd love to be able to draw like that."

"You just got to learn to see, Vinny. Then you'll be drawing like I do. Good morning, Dr. Sam."

"Morning, Nikki," said Dad, coming up. "Breakfast, Vinny?"

"I'm starving. But don't you think that's beautiful?"

Dad looked briefly at the drawing, not very interested.

"Pretty good," he said. "Come along, before the food is all gone."

As they were walking up toward the eating area she asked about Nikki.

"He said he was just here by accident, because he drew a dinosaur."

"I told you, there's only one paleontologist in the country. Watson Azikwe. You met him last night."

"The one with the gold chains?"

"That's him. But for reasons of national pride this has got to be a joint expedition, so we get landed with people like Nikki. It's not such a bad idea, to my mind. I'd much rather have someone we can teach, like Nikki, than some half-taught chap who wants to prove he's better than the rest of us. Nikki's being useful."

"Because he can draw?"

"Because he can see. Not much point in knowing a lot about fossils unless you can spot them in the first place. Locals are often superb at that—you know, herdsmen who think we're quite mad with our passion for old bones, but show them what you want and tell them there's money in it, and they'll spot things professionals might have missed."

"I'd really love to find a fossil."

They'd reached the eating area. Dr. Hamiska was sitting with his wife and Dr. Wessler, reading a document, but he must have heard what she said. He looked up at once.

"You shall, Vinny, you shall," he said. "I'll see to it personally."

Dad was pretending not to have heard. He was still walking toward the table with the food laid out on it.

"In fact," said Dr. Hamiska a little more loudly, "you shall do that this morning. There's a site I want to have another look at. We'll leave immediately after you've finished your breakfast, before it gets too hot."

"Oh . . . I really want to watch Dad taphonoming. Nobody else has got a father who's a taphonomist."

"And you actually know what a taphonomist does?"

"Yes, of course. I looked it up in the library. He uncovers fossils very carefully and then he tries to work out exactly how the animal died and what happened to the bones after that. Is that right?"

"Pretty good, Vinny. It's what I've been doing all my life, only now they have a fancy name for it. Well, you can watch your father working as soon as there's that kind of work to be done. Is that all right with you, Sam? Jane and I will take Vinny off your hands while you're finishing that report."

Dad had come back with a bowl of muesli and a mug of coffee.

"Where are you proposing to take her?" he asked flatly.

"I want to have another look at that outcrop beyond H8."

"You'll be wasting your time. Michael and I went over it a month ago. There may have been something there once, but it's all been eroded down the hill."

"I know, I know. I just have a feeling about it."

"You'll still be wasting your time. If you don't trust me, you might at least trust Michael."

"And I also want to take some samples of those tuffs. They're the clearest sequence we've got. All right?"

"It's your time, and it'll mean Vinny sees something of

the country, I suppose. Don't forget she's not acclima-
tized."

"Jane will lend her a parasol."

Dad grunted and moved off to another table. Vinny
fetched herself cornflakes, a banana, and orange juice and
joined him.

"I don't have to go with him if you don't want me to,"
she muttered.

"You might as well now."

"It's all right. I'm not going to let him take me over."

"It isn't just that—it's all sorts of things. I bet you, for
instance, he will find something. Or if he doesn't, Jane will
—she's got a fantastic eye. And then he'll come back and
laugh at me for having missed it. Oh, never mind. The
important thing is for you to keep out of the sun as much
as you can, wear sunglasses, slap on gallons of lotion, and
don't be ashamed of telling people if you're finding it too
much."

"I've got a big floppy hat too. I'll be all right. And we'll
go taphonoming this evening, right?"

"If you like."

Then

Next morning Li hunted early for food, and was lucky. With Iggi she levered a flat rock aside on the floor of the bay and found a large crab which they cracked open and shared before any of the adult males were around to come and take their prey off them. Then she went out again to the spit, to wait for the dolphin. She was sure it would come, and it did.

They played and danced as they'd done the day before. Since the dolphin was so much the better swimmer, so made for the single element of water, it played with her as an older child might play with a younger one, teaching it an easy game, patient with its mistakes and clumsiness. Li's wonder and joy were no less than before. Laughter burst from her mouth whenever she surfaced, while underwater she became aware that the sea was not silent, but full of whistlings and clicks, which seemed to come from the dolphin itself.

Then it swam suddenly away, and she realized that there were other whistlings coming from far off, which it seemed to have gone to answer. She waited in the water unalarmed, sure that it would not have left her in danger. She heard the noises returning, watched underwater, saw shadows move, and all at once found herself in the middle of a large shoal racing in panic past her. She missed two strikes but grabbed a fish at her third try and surfaced. A big dolphin arched past, ignoring her, and then three more close behind it. The water foamed around her with the rush of their passing, and then a final dolphin rose and tried to take the still-struggling fish from her hand. She let go and sank beside the dolphin as it sank, hearing the whistles of the hunt recede.

The dolphin waited, impatient. Why didn't she join the hunt? it seemed to be saying. She slid her arm around it and gestured underwater toward the shore. Again it understood and let her lie beside it, streamlining her body along its flank, as it leapt through the waves. Half the tribe were out on the spit, watching and pointing. Presh dived and swam to meet her, but as he approached, the dolphin bucked itself loose from her grasp and swam off.

This was bad for Presh. To maintain his dominance he couldn't let anyone else achieve triumphs which he couldn't either outdo or somehow counter. If Li had been an adult male Presh would at once have displayed at him and faced him down, and if necessary fought him. But Li was a child, and children didn't have that kind of triumph. There was no ritual, no mechanism, for dealing with what she had done.

Presh solved the problem first by patrolling the shark-watch line and sending the watchers ashore. Then, watched by the tribe, he turned toward the open sea, sank below the surface, and shot his body back up until he was visible to the waist. As he reached the top he let out a yell of challenge, and as he came down he slapped his palms against the surface to force two arching sprays of foam

away from him. At once the tribe understood what he was
doing. This was the first stage of a contest for dominance
between a leader and a challenger, but they had never seen
it used as Presh was using it now.

He leapt again and again, but at last turned and gestured
to the watchers to prepare for the next stage of the ritual.
Puzzled but obedient they went and lined the shallows of
the bay, facing the shore. Presh came last of all, swimming
and then wading straight to where Li was waiting appre-
hensively beside Ma-ma. She ducked herself down until
her long hair floated out around her and only the curve of
her spine showed above water, the gesture of total submis-
sion. He seized her beneath the arms, lifted her up, and
strode ashore. Watched in silence and alarm by the rest of
the tribe, he turned and raised her to sit on his shoulder.
Startled, she grabbed his hair to stop herself falling. He
punched his free hand into the air, let out a bellowing
laugh, and began the triumph dance.

He was telling the tribe that he, Presh, Leader, had sent
his niece Li out to ride in deep water with the dolphins,
and now they were to welcome her home. So he made her
triumph into his triumph, telling them to praise both Li
and himself as bringers of wonders.

Now they knew what to do. As Presh moved with a
dancelike strut along the shore, turning and stamping on
the rocks and punching the air with his hand, they answered with cries of *Praise!* and as he passed they struck the
water with their palms, shooting arches of spray over the
pair of them, a salute of glittering foam through which
their shining black bodies moved in glory. Li kept her grip
on Presh's hair but with her free hand punched the air,
copying his gesture, timing her movements to his, so that
the parade was for her like a continuation of the dance
with the dolphin, as she moved with a big, strong creature

through its element. It struck no one as strange or wrong that she should share in a Leader triumph, though nothing like this had ever happened before.

Normally the tribe would have stayed for at least one more day at that bay, but as the sun lost its heat Presh gave signals for a move and took them off northward under a waxing moon. Perhaps he felt that he couldn't afford to let Li dance again with the dolphin and not be allowed to join in himself. Or perhaps it was a vaguer feeling, that the bay was for the moment awesome, and that it would be easier for the tribe to go elsewhere until they had come to terms with what had happened.

Next morning Riff's family cornered a large eel. It took several adults to heave aside the boulder under which it had hidden and to wrestle it ashore, so Presh had time to take charge, and then to control the shareout. Eels being slow to die and too rubbery to tear apart, this meant passing the squirming body around and letting the favored ones gnaw what they could from it. Presh spat out his first mouthful and gave it to Li, an extraordinary honor for a child.

That night Ma-ma started her labor. The females gave birth in water, usually just before dawn. The mother would leave the sleeping tribe and go with one close friend down into the shallows, where the friend would help with the birth and lift the baby to the surface for its first breath of air. Sometimes a younger female, not quite ready for mating, would go and watch, to learn how the thing was done. It would be a year before Li reached that age but Ma-ma took her all the same, and clutched her to her side as she pushed the infant out of her body, while Hooa caught him and guided him to the surface to wail in the dawn air. His birth fur was sleek as a sealskin. His mouth in the bare, wrinkled face whimpered and sucked and his hands grasped and grasped at emptiness.

Ma-ma took him as soon as she was ready and put him to her nipple. As he started to suck she placed a tress of her hair against each tiny pink palm. Immediately the fingers closed and held. That was right. It was a good birth, all that a birth should be. Hooa was muttering *Joy, Praise,* and Li was doing so too, without noticing, entranced with happiness and wonder. She had never seen a birth close up. The child was inside the mother—all the tribe knew that —and when her time came she went into the sea and pushed it out of her and there it was. This had seemed no more strange or surprising than the swarming of the shrimp at full moon. It happened. There was no need to explain it.

But now Li stared at the baby as if it had been she herself who'd just been thrust into the world. Where had he come from? The mystery wasn't the neat body, with fur to keep it warm through the chill of night. Ma-ma had some-how made that inside herself after mating with Tong. (The tribe were aware that females like Liai who refused to mate had no children.) The mystery was the person. This new other. Himself. How could he be made? If he wasn't made, where had he been? How did the lips know to suck, the fingers to grasp Ma-ma's locks so that when she was foraging in the water, using both hands, the baby would float safely beside her?

The baby sucked, then slept. Ma-ma crooned. Li squat-ted beside her, still as a rock in the trance of wonder. Perhaps he had come out of the sea. Yes, perhaps the dol-phins had brought him from the place where the sun rose, and when Ma-ma had pushed the body out of her he had slid, transparent as a shrimp, under the water and in through the mouth, to make its home in the body like a hermit crab taking over a new shell. Perhaps.

Carrying a baby with its birth fur still on it brought Ma-ma great prestige. She was already one of the senior females, but now for a while she became the second most respected person in the tribe, after Presh. Females, and some males, competed to hold the baby. Tong brought food and a birth present, a shining shell. The shell had a hole in it, so Li threaded some of Ma-ma's hairs through it and tied them so that it dangled against her shoulder. The hairs soon wore through, but Li experimented and invented a form of plaiting which lasted well. The ornament was much admired and added to Ma-ma's prestige.

The next child was born in a family not close to Li's, but still she was woken and went down to watch over the birth. The father had already found a piece of shell with a hole in it for Li to make into a neck ornament like Ma-ma's. Over the months this became a custom in the tribe, something they did because it felt right, as though it had always been done. The plaits tended to wear through at about the time the babies lost their birth fur, which added to the feeling of rightness.

Probably Li was the only one who ever thought back to how the custom had started.

Now:
Monday Morning

Mrs. Hamiska was a small, quiet woman with a flat face and pale blue eyes. Her skin looked like soft leather. She said nothing the whole journey, but she didn't get much chance because Dr. Hamiska barely stopped talking. The landscape reeled by, gray-brown, flat, battered with heat, with hardly a tree, hardly a tussock of grass, just here and there patches of low, thorny scrub which looked dead but in fact had tiny leaves like fish scales. These were the badlands Dad had talked about, and the scrub was almost the only plant able to grow there. Again, it wasn't the Africa you saw on TV.

Vinny sat in the back of the jeep, craning forward to listen to Dr. Hamiska explaining about the badlands. This was where they had found most of their fossils. When the plain which you saw from the camp had been sea, and the hills where the camp was had been an island, this had been the channel between the island and the mainland. Then, slowly, the land had risen, and it had become a great marsh, and creatures had lived and died there, leaving their bones in the marsh. Rivers had fed the marsh, bringing down silt from the hills, layer after layer after layer, covering the bones. Then the coastline had risen, cutting the marsh off from the sea, and slowly it had dried out, evaporated, becoming saltier and saltier as it did so. It was badlands still because of the salt. The plates of the earth had ground against each other and there had been earthquakes, tilting the edges of the plain into new young hills, where the layers of silt compacted into clay and fresh soft rock, while the buried bones became fossils within them.

Time had streamed by, hundreds of thousands of seasons, wet, dry, wet, dry, wet, dry, each wet softening the surface of the earth and each dry baking it hard again. Sometimes rain washed whole mountainsides away. Sometimes things barely changed at all.

"I've seen sites which were explored thirty years before," said Dr. Hamiska. "You could still see the old beer cans. But not one new fossil had been exposed—barely a millimeter of erosion in thirty years. But then a man I know was digging out a dinosaur from the side of a gully. Tanzania, this was. A dinosaur can be a big thing—you don't get it done in a day. He'd got it half done when there was a thunderstorm and a flash flood down the gully, and the whole dinosaur was washed away. He'd lost it completely."

"He must have been furious."

"Not at all. The flood had exposed an even better specimen below the first one. Now, look, that's where we're heading for."

They had been steadily approaching the range of hills which millions of years before had been the coast of mainland Africa. From far off they'd seemed to rise sheer from the desolate flat plain, but now Vinny could see that there were foothills reaching out, brown and hummocky, below the ragged peaks. Dr. Hamiska pointed toward a shapeless lump rising like a small island almost straight ahead, separate from the rest of the range.

"Was it an island in the marsh?" said Vinny.

"It wasn't anything. What seems to have happened was that there was a series of earthquakes which made those lower hills. They're a real geological mess, but for some reason to do with the underlying rock structure that outcrop was pushed up all of a piece, so that where the old strata are exposed they lie in the same order as that in which they were laid down. I'm not a professional geologist, but I know enough for my immediate purposes. If I can get a complete sequence of strata deposition in this locality, then I may be able to match up partial sequences which I find elsewhere."

"Like tree-ring dating."

"Exactly. For instance, the skull May Anna is working on was found in association with a layer of tuff—that's fossilized ash from a volcanic eruption. There are a whole series of tuffs in the strata, and I'm hoping that by sequencing the tuffs on this outcrop I can find out which is the one the skull belongs to, and hence get a line on the dating."

"Are there any fossils here?"

He laughed.

"There *were* fossils here, Vinny. Some were brought to us from a point at the foot of the outcrop, eroded down the hill. Your father and a very experienced African did a survey, and they say there are no more to be found, but you and Jane and I are going to prove them wrong."

He laughed again, but Vinny could hear it was only half a joke. Then he had to stop talking. They had been traveling so far along a sort of track, reasonably level, winding between the scrub and pits and hummocks of the plain.

Now he left it, changed into low gear, and edged down into what looked like a dry riverbed with soft, gritty sand in the bottom. There was no track at all on the other side. Still in low gear he took the jeep twisting and lurching along below the outcrop, so that Vinny had to clutch the back of the seats, though Mrs. Hamiska sat calmly swaying, with her hands folded in her lap, as if on a church outing.

They stopped and climbed out, and now the heat of Africa smote them. Already, before they'd left the camp, Vinny had found it so hot that she'd been picking her way around through patches of shade rather than cross direct through the sunlit areas. The journey had been better with the breeze of movement blowing in under the jeep's canvas roof. The badlands were hotter than she'd dreamed, even under the parasol, the green sun umbrella which Mrs. Hamiska had lent her. (She'd thought she'd feel silly using it, but it made sense now.) Mrs. Hamiska wore a sleeveless cotton frock and a straw hat, still looking as if she were on a church outing, while Dr. Hamiska put on an old corduroy cap with its peak turned backward to cover his neck. He should have looked like a complete clown, but he didn't.

"The eroded finds were a couple of hundred yards along that way," he said. "We'll have a look there later. But first I'd like you to come and help me measure the tuffs on that section of exposed rock. That's where they're clearest."

He pointed up the slope to the left. The hill was a dark rusty brown with yellower patches, and here and there the dead-looking thorn bushes. The odd boulder jutted out of the soil, but the only real difference was a section of low cliff two thirds of the way up. He was starting to climb toward it when Mrs. Hamiska bent and reached in under one of the thorn bushes. Vinny hadn't even noticed her looking. She rose with something in her hand.

"Look at this, Joe," she said.

He turned and took the object from her, chuckling as he held it up between finger and thumb. From the ones she'd seen under the awning Vinny recognized it as a fossil tooth.

"Sam didn't find everything, then," he said. "That's about four million. Four point two. Somewhere around there."

"It makes my skin prickle, thinking about all that time," said Vinny.

"And so it should. I tell my students that the past is an immense ocean which we can neither sail on nor dive down into. We are stuck to our shore, which is the present. Out on the surface we can see the past of the history books, the storms and the shipwrecks, but of what happened in the far past, down in the deeps of that ocean, we have nothing to go on except the shells and bones it chooses to wash up at our feet. Why do we bother, then? What does it matter? It matters because that ocean is where we come from. Those seas are in our blood."

His voice throbbed. If he hadn't told her, Vinny might still have guessed that this was part of a lecture.

"I suppose you've got to be lucky to find the right things," she said.

"Indeed you have. I know experts in my field who've never once had the excitement of picking up a hominid fossil. Others seem unable to step off an airplane without finding something new. That's why I believe in luck. I seriously believe that there are some people who can call out across the ocean of time and summon it to wash its secrets to their feet. I am one, and for all I know you may be another."

He gazed at the four-million-year-old fragment in his

hand as if he were praying to it, using it for his summoning magic, then gave it back to Mrs. Hamiska.

"See if you can spot where it came from, darling," he said. "Come on, Vinny."

They started up the slope. It wasn't much of a climb, but sweat streamed down Vinny's body, making her clothes cling and pull, and she needed a rest halfway up. Looking back over the gray, roasting desert she tried to imagine it when it had been a marshy lake, steaming under this sun, with rivers running in and pigs rootling in the reed beds, and other creatures, creatures who were almost people, perhaps, making their camp at the water's edge . . . Mrs. Hamiska was drifting along the slope halfway down, quiet as cloud shadow, with her head bent like a nun in a cloister. Vinny climbed on and found Dr. Hamiska measuring and sketching the slanting rock layers in the cliff. He didn't really need her to help him, only to be there so that he had someone to talk to, to teach.

"You see this layering, how it's tilted? This gray band? That's tuff—remember? And here, just above it, these coarser particles, and then these finer ones and then this thin band of tuff again. So we had a minor volcanic eruption followed by a dry spell—not much flow in the rivers, you see—and then a wetter spell bringing heavier particles down from the hills, and then a really big eruption. That's a very characteristic section. If it turns up elsewhere in the area I shall know where it comes in the sequence. Now I'm going to see if I can hack out some good unweathered crystals from the tuff. There's a technique called potassium-argon dating . . ."

"Jane's found something."

He swung to look. Mrs. Hamiska was kneeling now, and prodding carefully at the earth with a narrow trowel.

"You want to go and see?" he said. "Come and fetch me if it's anything worthwhile."

Vinny found Mrs. Hamiska using a painter's brush to clear the earth she'd loosened around a shapeless small lump. She glanced up at Vinny's approach.

"Yes, he'd better come," she said.

Dr. Hamiska was still watching, so Vinny simply waved and he came loping down like a schoolboy. He rushed past Vinny, knelt and took the trowel from Mrs. Hamiska and prodded it vigorously into the earth around the lump, not bothering to use the brush, hoicking chunks of clay out. In a few minutes he had the thing free and was nudging the last bits of clay off with his thumbs.

"There!" he said, holding it triumphantly up. To Vinny it looked like a bit of twisted dead branch.

"What is it?" she said.

"A lower mandible. Some kind of small deer, perhaps. Look, that's where one of the molars fitted, and another here. Not in itself very exciting, but the point is that it was buried in the original matrix, so there's every chance we've now got the level from which the tooth Jane found was eroded down. Have you brought a cord, darling? Excellent. And a peg and a hammer. Good. Now, Vinny, go back up, oh, to about where I was working, and we'll see if we can use the angle of strata in the cliff to get a line on how they might run down here . . ."

Vinny toiled back up the hill, trailing the line, too excited to notice the heat. Dr. Hamiska strode up and down lifting the line clear of obstacles, then moved to a point where he could compare its angle to that of the rock strata. From there he shouted instructions. When he was satisfied Vinny hammered her peg in and tied the line taut. Using it as a guide, the Hamiskas worked along inch by inch, studying every bump or nubble in the earth. Mrs. Hamiska found two splinters of bone, leg probably, and Dr. Hamiska found the tooth of a pigmy hippo. All three were below the cord, so Vinny had to climb and adjust the top peg. She came back to find him burrowing at the hillside like a dog, showering loose earth down the slope.

"Look!" he cried. "Here's our tuff! It's the same one, I'll bet my life on it. And the finds are right on top of it. Now . . . !"

Mrs. Hamiska was watching him, amused. Her way of smiling was to try not to, which made her purse her lips as if she were trying to spit out a grape seed. He jumped to his feet, flung his arms around her, and kissed her on both cheeks, lifting her clean off the ground.

"Put me down, please, Joe," she said. "We're not twenty anymore."

She didn't sound disapproving. As often before, with other married people who seemed totally different from each other, Vinny wondered how they'd managed to stay together when Mom and Dad hadn't. At the back of the hole Dr. Hamiska had dug she saw a faint band of gray crossing the yellowish earth. Then, because her eyes knew what they were looking for, she realized she could see the same band right out on the surface, slanting down nearly parallel to the cord. It was so faint that she had to be standing directly on its line to see it, and looking back up the slope to where it should have run on till it reached a large flat-topped rock she couldn't see it at all. When she climbed and looked down from the rock it was there, all the way to her feet. It was something to do with the angle of the light, probably.

"I can see your tuff, Joe," she called. "If you stand here . . ."

He rushed to join her and stare, rushed back for more pegs, marked the new line, and prowled along it, snorting with excitement and effort, as if he could bully the hidden fossils out into the open by pure willpower. Mrs. Hamiska was already digging at something else. Vinny stared at the earth beside the rock but could see nothing. She knelt and moved her fingertips across the ground, closing her eyes, concentrating on the task of feeling. Ah. No, it was only a pebble. So was that. A faint ridge, like the cut end of a Scotch tape reel which you can feel but not see. She picked at it with a fingernail. It was harder than clay.

"Please, is this something?" she called, keeping her finger on the spot, fearful of losing it.

Mrs. Hamiska stopped working to come and look and feel.

"Yes, that's probably a fossil," she said. "Broken, I think."

"What is it?"

"Oh, I can't tell you yet. Do you want to dig it out yourself?"

"Is that all right? I'd love to."

"I brought a trowel and a brush for you. Be patient. Don't lever against the fossil—they can be very fragile."

"Oh, thank you! Isn't this exciting!"

Mrs. Hamiska smiled her mysterious smile. Her eyes were invisible behind her sunglasses, so Vinny couldn't tell if she was smiling at her or with her. She helped Vinny prop her parasol on the rock to cast a useful patch of shade and returned to her own work.

Gently Vinny eased the trowel tip into the soil and levered the first crumb of clay free. There'd been no need to tell her to be patient. This was the sort of job she did best, with its bit-at-a-time delicacy, and the way her hands learned the nature of what they were working with, so that they seemed to know almost at once how far to push the trowel in, and how to twist and lever so that another fragment came cleanly away from the ancient bone. Her world narrowed to a square foot of hillside. She forgot heat and thirst and the ache of crouching. Her whole being became the slave of the bone.

It seemed to be thin and flat and to lie almost level in the hill so that its left edge actually broke through the sloping line of tuff. The outer edge had been snapped off where it reached the surface, and the right corner, about half a square inch, was cracked and loose from the main bit. She was working not down but sideways into the hill, digging out a hollow like a miniature quarry with the bone as its floor. Dr. Hamiska's boots crunched on the rock above her. She rose to let him see what she'd been doing.

"That's great," he said. "We'll have to employ you full-time."

"What is it? Do you know?"

"A fragment of scapula, I think. Shoulder blade to you, Vinny. Some fair-sized beast. Don't try and lever it out or you'll break it—you'll have to undercut it first. Look how the sequence runs at the back there—that's beautiful."

"Do you think it was killed in the eruption?"

"Could be, could be. Your father's here to answer questions like that. The ash would have been soft, mind you, so the creature could have died after the eruption and then the bones partly embedded themselves. Lend me your trowel, will you? I could get a column of the sequence out there—something to show them on Thursday. Blind them with science, eh?"

Still chuckling, he forced the blade vertically down at the back of Vinny's quarry, as if he were cutting the first slice out of a birthday cake. The slice broke in two when he eased it out but he fitted the pieces together and laid them carefully out on the slope.

"Now if you'll ask Jane for a bag and a label," he said, "and then we'll— Hold it! Hold everything!"

He pushed his sunglasses onto his forehead and stared into the slice-shaped cut he had made. His breath hissed between closed teeth. With Vinny's brush he swept the loose bits from a pale lump which had been exposed on one side of the cut, just above the tuff. He took a magnifying glass from his shirt pocket and gazed intently through it.

"Jane," he called. "Come here a moment."

He'd changed. A moment before he'd been the friendly old professor showing off to the visitor. Now he'd forgotten she was there. Mrs. Hamiska came and crouched beside him. Every line of their bodies expressed enthralled excitement. Two terriers at the same rabbit hole.

"Oh, yes," said Mrs. Hamiska. "I think so. I really do think so."

"Whoopee!" bellowed Dr. Hamiska, standing and flinging his cap into the air. It landed halfway down the hillside.

"Let me have a go," said Mrs. Hamiska. "You're a bit too excited."

Without waiting for an answer she started to chip the clay away from the other side of the cut. Vinny fetched Dr. Hamiska's cap, and then helped him measure and peg out an area around the find. Standing on the rock he began to draw a sketch map. By now Mrs. Hamiska had opened the cut enough for Vinny to see that the fossil was a stubby cylindrical bone with a bulge at each end.

"Is it part of someone's hand?" she said.

"Their foot, Vinny, their foot!" crowed Dr. Hamiska. "It's a distal phalanx—a toe bone to you, Vinny. You are looking at the left big toe of a creature that walked on its hind legs five million years ago! It's going to be datable by the tuff! And either my name's not Joseph Seton Hamiska or the rest of the skeleton is all there, right under our feet! The oldest fossil hominid yet found! I knew it! I knew it! I knew the moment I woke up that this was my day, and this was going to be the place! Whoopee!"

You could have heard his shouts a mile across the plain. Mrs. Hamiska straightened and watched him, like Mom watching Colin and the boys let the sea run into the moat of their sandcastle, yelling with triumph as it swirled around their ramparts.

"I think you'd better get Sam out here, darling," she said.

"Yes, yes, of course. And Fred and the others—as many witnesses as we can. We don't want any nonsense this time. I'll call them up."

He charged down the hill toward the jeep, where he'd left the two-way radio, but halfway down he stopped and turned.

"Vinny!" he shouted. "Didn't I tell you, the moment I set eyes on you, you were going to bring us luck!"

Then

Nobody liked Greb. He was a big, surly young male who didn't keep to the rules. A while ago he'd broken Nuhu's arm. She and some other children had been playing a splashing game around a rock pool when Greb had settled near them with a clam he'd found and a rock to hammer it open. Nuhu had wheedled for a bit of clam. A normal male would have barked a *Go away,* but Greb had shoved her hard enough to knock her flat, so that she'd banged her head on a rock and started to howl. Greb in sheer bad temper had brought his hammerstone down on her outstretched arm, snapping the bone above the wrist.

Mirn had tried to give Greb a hiding, but Greb had refused to be cowed. That was when Mirn had started to lose his leadership, giving Presh the chance to take over. Nuhu's arm had mended, crooked and short, so that later, when she'd begun to wonder about things, Li had become interested in it, and when Nuhu would let her had touched and felt and stroked it, comparing it with the feel of the bone in her own arm, wondering how a bone could mend itself, and whether, if it happened again to someone, she could help the bone to mend straight . . . you'd have to hold it straight with something, for a long time . . . difficult . . .

Now the children gave Greb a wide berth, and the adults had as little to do with him as they could. He paid no attention, and foraged wherever anyone else was finding food, often snatching their catch from them. Males sometimes did this, but Greb seemed to prefer to steal food rather than find it for himself. And when the tribe settled down for the night, he made a point of choosing a place where the bodies lay thickest and forcing himself down among them. He refused to do shark watch.

Though still young, Greb was as strong as any male in the tribe, and if he'd known how to make allies, everyone would have realized that one day he'd become Leader. Presh was quite different, friendly and easygoing. He liked to visit the families every day, and not just because they would offer him any food they'd found, out of deference. Usually he'd take a mouthful and give the rest back. If children disturbed him while he was snoozing in the shallows, his *Go away* was more laughter than anger, and they weren't afraid of him. Only when his dominance was threatened did he make the hair on his head and nape stand out, and snarl and bare his teeth, and hunch his shoulders, big-muscled from swimming. Then he could look really dangerous.

When Greb had made trouble before, Presh had taken Tong and Kerif to help give him a thrashing, reinforcing their authority over their own groups of families, so though one of them would have been the natural challenger, they remained content as things were. In fact a challenge from any male in the tribe would have been a surprise, so complete was his acceptance. That it should be

Greb—young, disliked, without any authority beyond his own strength—broke all the rules.

A challenge should have been built up to in a series of confrontations, testing the Leader's self-confidence and his support from the rest of the tribe. It should come like the start of the rains, slowly, with tension in the air and days of waiting and far-off thunder, until everyone was ready for the outburst, longing for it, to get it over.

No one realized at first that anything was happening. Greb chose a place where a headland ended in a series of shelving rocks, with deep fissures between them. A seaweed grew here whose young fruiting-fronds were good to eat. Juicy seasnails fed on the weed, and crayfish could be poked out of crannies, so the tribe was spread along the headland, mostly out of sight of each other, foraging between the rocks. Many of them missed the challenge ritual and arrived to watch only when the actual fighting had begun.

This may have been clever of Greb. A popular leader drew confidence from the support of the tribe, and at first Presh was partly deprived of that. But some, including Li, saw everything that happened. Ma-ma was still carrying her baby and so had a right to the best feeding places, and Li foraged alongside her. She had eaten as much as she wanted, and was now floating in the gentle swell, eyes closed, looking as if she were asleep but in fact wondering about the dolphins. They hadn't returned, but they still haunted her thoughts. Last night, waking on a roosting ledge and seeing the moonlit sky, she'd found herself wondering why the sun was hot and the moon cold, why the moon changed its shape and the sun didn't, and then she'd slept and dreamed of dolphins playing with the moon and sun. Now, remembering that dream, she told herself that they all came out of the sea, the dolphins as well as the sun and the moon and the stars. Perhaps they all come from the same place. Perhaps one day a dolphin would take her there. It couldn't be far, at the speed a dolphin swam.

A hoot of challenge broke into her musings and she rolled over to look. A few yards away Greb shot vertically out of the water, visible almost to his knees, bellowing as he reached the top of his leap and flailing his spread arms down as he sank back to arch two huge jets of spray at his opponent. It was a terrific display. Li paddled swiftly clear —fighting males had no time to watch out for children.

Her move brought Presh into view, rising, bellowing, flailing in rhythmic answer. His voice was far more commanding than Greb's but his leaps not quite so high. It didn't cross Li's mind that he wouldn't punish Greb easily enough. He was in his prime and had the whole tribe behind him.

The challenge ritual was exhausting. (It was meant to be, so that if it came to a full-blooded fight, both combatants would already be very tired and the weaker would quickly give in. That way neither of them would get seriously hurt.) Gradually the tribe gathered to watch. Li moved to be close to Ma-ma among the rows of bobbing heads. The baby floated asleep by Ma-ma's shoulder with his hands twined fast in her hair, and occasionally she'd scoop up a little water and wet the smooth round face. She looked worried. Presh was her brother and they had always been close.

At last Presh decided that he wasn't going to overawe Greb by mere display and he would have to fight him. He climbed out onto a flat platform of rock and fell into his combat pose, erect, arms braced, fingers half clenched like the talons of a sea eagle, teeth bared between snarling lips. He shook his hair around him so that it would dry into a

glossy black mane and crest. He bellowed, challenging
Greb to match his display.

Greb didn't bother. Neither the display, nor the fact that
the whole watching tribe were on Presh's side, seemed to
affect him at all. He climbed out on the other side of the
platform and immediately flew straight at Presh. The impact flung them both off the rock and into the water.

The tribe yelled their excitement. Challenge fights were
a break from the day-to-day. They wanted to see Greb
humiliated and punished, but they wanted a good fight
first. It would add to Presh's prestige if he won with cour-
age.

The combatants rose apart, climbed out, and rushed at
each other. This time they fell on the rock and rolled
about, locked together, biting and clawing. They separated, stood, circled, grappled, and fell once more, rolling
across the rock till they tumbled over the edge, bouncing
off a jut of barnacled rock on their way down. Greb was
underneath and must have caught the side of his head on a
jag, because when he climbed out blood was pouring
down his neck and shoulder. Such a hurt would have allowed any normal challenger to give in without loss of
prestige, but Greb ignored it and rushed at Presh once
more.

The nature of the tribe's interest changed. Now they
realized that for Greb no rules applied. This could be a
fight to the death.

The pair battled repetitively on, exhausted, bruised, cut,
blood-smeared. Greb's first wound was still the only serious one. The sea would wash him clean, but before the
fighters grappled again his neck and side would be streaked
with scarlet and then as they fought the blood would
blotch both of them until they tumbled once more into
the sea. Greb was weakening faster than Presh, who now at

the start of each bout fell into his challenge pose again, inviting Greb to submit. Greb ignored the offer and every time flung himself into the attack, blinder, madder, ever more hopeless. But still he fought on.

At last the end came. Once more they climbed onto the rock, once more Presh took up his pose, once more Greb attacked. They stood wrestling together. Presh began to force Greb to the edge, meaning to fling him into the sea and stand in triumph over him. The movement stopped. The rock surface was invisible to the watchers below, but they could see that Presh had caught his foot in something. For a moment he and Greb poised together until Presh in his effort to free his foot unbalanced them both and Greb wrestled him down. The whole tribe heard the leg bone snap.

Presh screamed. Greb rose dazed and gasping, wiped the blood from his eyes and stared around, not understanding that the fight was over, looking to see where his enemy would rise from the water. Then he saw him lying moaning at his feet. He bent. Presh yelled with agony as his foot was wrenched from the fissure that had trapped it, and was still screaming when Greb tumbled him into the water.

Strength seemed to flow back into Greb. Still bleeding, he stood erect, surveyed the platform and saw that it was too small, too uneven, and too high above the water for a good triumph ritual. The tribe watched him, dazed, seemingly without minds of their own, and when he made a gesture of command and plunged into the water they followed him, but reluctantly and with many stragglers, down beside the steep, dark cliffs to a shingly bay between that headland and the next.

Ma-ma stayed with Presh, buoying him up and crooning comfort. He had fainted now, and without her help might have drowned. Li took the baby while with Hooa's help

Ma-ma towed Presh along after the others. By the time they reached the bay Greb was well into his triumph dance.

Lined along the shallows the tribe cried *Praise* and dutifully flung their arches of water toward him, some so half-heartedly that the splash barely reached his ankles. If he noticed he would pause in his dance and come menacingly down, frightening the offenders into showing him more respect. This had happened twice before he reached the place where Ma-ma had joined the line.

The baby had woken and was crying. Li was trying to soothe him, Ma-ma and Hooa were busy with Presh. None of them attempted a splash. Greb glared at them and came stamping down. Alerted by the sudden hush Ma-ma looked up, saw him coming, and then slowly, deliberately, turned her back on him. Without thought Li copied her.

Greb bellowed and gave Ma-ma a buffet that sent her floundering. He seized Li by the nape. She screamed and dropped the baby. She thought he was about to fling her onto the shingle and trample her, but instead he crammed her onto his shoulder and stamped back up the beach to continue his parade, just as Presh had paraded with her after her dance with the dolphin. He would show the whole tribe that Li and her prestige were now his, to command and control.

She was terrified. She screamed and struggled. He struck at her with his free hand and she screamed louder still. Ma-ma was there, facing him, with Hooa beside her, both yelling, more of them, females, and then males, all crowding out of the water, thronging around Greb, screaming their outrage, refusing his triumph after all. It was over. They wouldn't accept him. He had broken the challenge rules, won the fight by an accident, struck a mother who carried a baby still in its birth fur, tried to own and control Li, who belonged to them all. He was not their leader.

Being Greb, he tried to fight them all, but they were too many and too angry. The crowd milled to and fro. Li rocked above it, yelling with terror and clutching Greb's mane to keep herself from falling. He loosed his hold on her to fight, and then she was grabbed from behind and wrenched free and passed back over the heads of the crowd, till they set her down. Whimpering, she staggered down to Ma-ma, who was crouched in the shallows, clutching her screaming baby to her. Presh lay inert beside her, half in and half out of the water. Shuddering with sobs, Li clung to Ma-ma's side and watched the end of the fight.

The milling mass dwindled as the females worked themselves free, leaving the males to finish Greb off. The cliffs echoed and reechoed with yells and bellows. Some fell and were trampled on until they crawled free. Then the scrimmage stilled and moved apart, forming a ring around the single body which lay inert in the middle. Silence fell. Li thought they must have killed him, till he moved.

He rose to hands and knees, lifted his head, and snarled. His blood smeared his whole body. One eye stayed closed. Watched by the males he staggered to his feet and lurched toward Kerif as if he meant to start the fight again, but when Kerif moved aside he lurched on. The tribe watched him limp down the shingle and wade into the healing sea. Followed by their hoots of *Shame!* he swam awkwardly away, using only his left arm, out along the cliffs of the farther headland, and disappeared.

Now:
Monday
Afternoon

Vinny wasn't feeling well. It was partly the argument between Dad and Dr. Hamiska, and partly the heat. The heat was appalling. The sun seared down onto the windless hillside and then seemed to bounce back up under her parasol, making her feel she wasn't in the shade at all. The plan had been to go back to the camp for lunch and rest under the awnings till it got cooler, but instead everyone had rushed out to look at the new fossil, and now Dad and Dr. Hamiska were arguing about it.

Dad stood on one side of the little hole, his body stiff, his gestures short and tense. Dr. Hamiska lolled against the boulder on the other side, laughing with excitement half the time. Before Dad had arrived he'd lost patience with Mrs. Hamiska's finicky picking around the fossil, and had taken over in order to explore further into the hillside, hacking whole trowelfuls of clay out at a time. Just before Dad and the others had arrived he'd found a second fossil—in fact he'd broken it in half with the trowel, and now while he talked to Dad he kept fitting the two pieces together and turning them over to look at and then holding them up as if they had magic in them, giving him power, like one of Tolkien's rings.

The others stood around listening to the argument. May Anna caught sight of Vinny and came across.

"You don't look too good," she said.

"I'm all right, but it's so hot, and I wish they'd stop arguing. What's it all about?"

"It's about what happens next. This bone you found . . ."

"I *didn't* find it! I wish Joe would stop saying I did. He found it. It's just a way of getting at Dad."

"I'm afraid Joe's like that. And he's dead sure now that the rest of the skeleton is lying there right in the hillside, just waiting to be dug out, and Sam's telling him to take it slow."

"But he's got to, hasn't he?"

"Sure, but it's a question how slow. We've got a couple of foot bones, right? But that doesn't mean there's a joined-up skeleton all neatly lying together. There could be just this foot, which a leopard or something brought here. But let's say it wasn't like that, and the body died in shallow water, then the water will have moved the bones around, and crayfish and crocs could have carried bits away. The bones could be spread out right through the hill. That's if they're there at all, because the body may have been lying the other way around, right? Out this way . . ."

May Anna gestured to show the imaginary strata spreading out beyond the hillside, as they would have been before the endless seasons had eroded them away.

". . . and those two bones are all that's left."

"But you've still got to look and see. I mean, it *might* be there."

"Right. But look how the strata run. Into the hill, see? There's a whole lot of hill to be cleared away to get at the one we want. Tons and tons and tons of earth. That means a labor force. How are we going to raise a labor force out here in the badlands? It'll take money, not just to pay them, but to get them here, feed them, and keep them here. Money Joe doesn't have—not till after Thursday, maybe, when the Craig people come. *Then* if he's got enough to show them, he can have all the labor he wants, and real funds for next year, and real good people who'll want to be with him next year. That's a lot to ask for on two little bones, Vinny. But if he could maybe find a leg bone, a knee . . . So he doesn't want Sam hanging about, waiting for a labor force before he starts serious digging. You see?"

Vinny nodded. She felt a need to explain something to May Anna. Making her bed that morning she'd found an old tube of eyeshadow, May Anna's color, wedged between the leg of the bed and the hut wall. Then on the earth floor she'd seen four square marks where the legs of another bed must have stood close alongside hers.

"I don't know Dad very well," she said. "My stepfather's lovely, but I just decided I wanted a dad of my own, like I've got a mom of my own. But it doesn't mean I've got to be with him all the time, or anything like that, only to know him a bit."

May Anna put her hand on Vinny's shoulder and held her comfortingly against her side.

"You're doing fine," she said. "Your dad's a great guy. He needs a daughter like you. It's good you came."

"Has he got to be enemies with Joe?"

"They're not enemies, but Joe's Joe. He's got to be always telling you he's there. Times he drives everyone crazy. Other times we'd be lost without him. Dee

Huntsman couldn't take Joe, so she said she was sick and went home . . ."

"She was your geologist?"

"Right. And okay, she got a bit sick, but if it hadn't been for Joe she'd have hung in. And look at today. We've a whole heap of things waiting decisions which only Joe can make, but instead he takes off blind after a hunch he's had in the night, and because he wants to show you how to find fossils, and we all know he's going to come back and decide things out of the top of his head, messing up work some guys have been doing for weeks. And he'll *still* do that. But what else? While he's off on this crazy jaunt with you he pokes into a bit of hillside and comes up with a proto-hominid foot bone, which any museum in the world would give its eyeteeth for! So we've all got to forgive him. Even Sam. Sam's as thrilled as the rest of us, if you want to know."

"I suppose he is, but . . ."

"You're like him that way, I guess. Excited he may be, but he's still got to do the job right, slowly, methodically, not missing a damn thing. Sam would never have bust that bone Joe's waving around now. They should've been a good team, you know. Sam needs Joe to raise the funding and find the sites, and Joe needs Sam to do the work right, so no one's going to argue about what they've found."

"I wish they'd stop arguing now."

"Just stopping . . . Any minute . . . Told you . . ."

Dr. Hamiska laughed and jumped to his feet and clapped Dad on the shoulder in a no-hard-feelings way, then started striding around the hillside, giving the rest of his team their orders. Dad came gloomily over.

"I guess Vinny's feeling the heat," said May Anna.

"No, I'm better," said Vinny. "What's going to happen now?"

"What's going to happen now is perfectly terrible," said Dad. "I suppose I accept it's got to be done in the circumstances. Joe wanted everyone out here, the cooks even, pretty well, hacking into the hillside at random, but I've persuaded him he'll have to make do with two trenches. I'll do one and Fred will do the other."

"What's so terrible about that?" said May Anna. "Fred's good."

"It isn't Fred. It's the results Joe wants by Thursday. I don't want to kill myself carting spoil around in this heat, so Fred and I are going to have to be out here by sunrise to get the heavy labor done while we can still stand it . . . I'm afraid you're not going to see much of me over the next few days, Vinny . . ."

"Vinny can help me," said May Anna. "We'll have fun."

"If Joe gives you a look-in," said Dad. "He seems to have persuaded himself that she's some kind of good-luck token."

"Well, I'm not," said Vinny. "I'm going to come and help you."

"I'd love you to," said Dad carefully. "But I'm not that easy to help. Most of it I've got to do myself."

"Then I'll just come," said Vinny. "It's all right. I won't be bored. I want to learn to draw like Nikki."

"Well . . ."

Dad was looking at May Anna, who wasn't saying anything. All Vinny knew was that she didn't want to be left at the camp being Dr. Hamiska's good-luck token. A new thought struck her.

"Couldn't we come and camp out here?" she said. "Just you and me and Dr. Wessler. Then you can start digging as soon as it's light and I'll cook your breakfast and . . ."

May Anna was laughing. Dad was looking around the parching landscape, miming disgust.

"I've never seen a less inviting spot for a fly camp," he said.

"Please, Dad."

"It's an idea," said May Anna. "It's only three nights, Sam, and you're always saying any fool can be uncomfortable in camp."

Dr. Hamiska came striding across.

"Okay," he said. "Ready, Sam? Let's get an awning rigged up for you to work under."

"Hang on a sec," said Dad. "I've been thinking. Since time's so short the best thing would be for me to set up a fly camp here . . ."

"Just what I was about to suggest. Good man."

"If May Anna can take the jeep back, with Vinny, Vinny can pack my gear while May Anna gets the other stuff together—there's the orange tent in the store, May Anna, and we'll need three beds . . ."

"Three?" said Dr. Hamiska.

"Fred, me, Vinny."

"You're not proposing to bring her out here?" said Dr. Hamiska.

His attitude had changed completely. A moment before he'd been easy, genial, friendly. Now he looked thoroughly put out, but couldn't at once think of an objection.

"It's all right," said Vinny. "I love camping. I won't get in the way."

"Vinny's here to see her father, don't forget," said May Anna.

"And Sam's here to get this other little lady out of the hill," said Dr. Hamiska, holding the broken fossil out to show what he meant. "It's a long way from civilization, Sam."

"We'll make a civilized fly camp," said Vinny.

Dr. Hamiska realized he wasn't going to win, and bellowed with laughter to show he didn't mind, but somehow it wasn't quite convincing. Dad and May Anna started to make a list of what he'd need, but when they roped Dr. Wessler in to join the discussion he refused to come to the fly camp. He said he'd got work at the main camp which he had to finish by Thursday. He'd do that this evening and come out with some of the others tomorrow to start the second trench. Dr. Hamiska accepted this without fuss.

It was midafternoon before they'd finished collecting everything that was needed for the fly camp. Vinny was tired, but feeling better. They made tea and drank it in the shade of a tree with feathery leaves and long, black dangling beans. Below them stretched the plain. The dusty air was tinged with orange and the sinking sun cast sidelong shadows, so that the flat-topped trees that dotted the plain were joined to their own shape in reverse—branches, trunk, shadow trunk, shadow branches—a single dark shape like a letter in a peculiar alphabet.

"Why wasn't Joe annoyed with Fred for not coming on the fly camp?" asked Vinny.

May Anna sighed.

"Well, I guess it was true what Fred said. He's got his classification model to get drawn out for the Craig people on Thursday. But then again Joe wouldn't get any satisfaction out of needling Fred. Fred's kind of slippery. He's like a fly you're trying to swat. Wham, but it's somewhere else already, you know? He just shrugs and smiles and doesn't react."

"Why don't you come?"

"I've got work too—my skull. Did I tell you I found another piece fitted this morning? And I hate camping too. This place is plenty primitive for me. I'm Minneapolis born and bred. I like streets. I say phooey to all that."

She gestured derisively at the plain, but Vinny knew she was joking. The plain was wonderful. In England you're doing well if you can see twenty miles, but here it could have been hundreds. The sky seemed huge. Far out across the tawny grassland something was moving, invisible itself but raising a haze of brown-gold dust. Not a car—it was too wide for that. A group of something, a whole herd, running, pounding up that dust with their hooves. Something must be hunting them. Lions? Wild dogs? Africa was incredibly old, Vinny thought. Animals had run from each other, hunted each other for millions of years. But even Africa changed. Once the plain had been sea and the badlands a sea channel and then a marsh. She tried to imagine it then. What sort of an island, what sort of a marsh? What creatures then? Pigs, crocodiles, small deer, all under the fierce African sun? And what sort of people? But her imagination wouldn't take hold. There was too much she didn't know.

May Anna laughed in the silence. Vinny looked at her.

"Just the way things pan out, I guess," said May Anna. "Were you nervous about coming?"

"A bit, I suppose. Mainly I was just excited."

"It was the other way around with Sam. He doesn't show he's excited, but, boy, was he nervous! How d'you think you're making out with him?"

"I don't know. It's difficult with Joe trying to take me over. We were doing all right, I thought, only this morning—well, I suppose I got a bit too interested in a book I was telling him about and he didn't approve of, and he started to go silent on me, and then, well, he sort of gave himself a shake and stopped. He told me to remember I'm my mother's daughter."

"Tell me about your mom. Sam won't. He says he doesn't know how to be fair to her, and he refuses to be unfair. That's typical of him, by the way. What's she like, Vinny?"

"Do you know any Old English sheepdogs?"

"Sure. Like that?"

"Not to look at. Outside she's small and neat, but inside she's sort of all-overish and shaggy and always bouncing and wanting to play and take part and involve everyone."

"That figures. What was the book?"

"It's by somebody called Elaine Morgan and . . ."

May Anna crowed with laughter.

"Have you read it?" said Vinny.

"Don't tell anyone, but yes. I took it on vacation, where no one would know who I was and I put a plain wrapper on it so no one would ask me about it . . ."

"Do *you* think it's nonsense?"

"No, not really. But I don't go around talking about it. I think she's wrong, but not crazy wrong. She deserves an answer."

"Why was Dad so upset?"

"Because you got excited and reminded him of your mom?"

"It wasn't just that. It was something to do with the book."

"That too. Sam's a real expert. He's spent, oh, twenty years getting his expertise. Bones are his thing. Mine too, though I'm not as good as he is. Yet. Just think what it's like having an amateur coming along and getting a lot of publicity saying the bones aren't that important and the experts are all wrong. Who's going to pay our salaries, who's going to fund expeditions like this, who's going to give us the respect and prestige we think we deserve, if people start taking her seriously? Those aren't our conscious motives. Consciously all we're interested in is the scientific truth, and we are—we really are! But, by golly, those other motives are there!"

"So I'd better not talk about it again? I really want to, but . . ."

May Anna didn't answer at once. Then she sighed.

"I don't know," she said. "I haven't figured Sam out. But if you want my advice, I'd say be what you are and talk about what you want to talk about. Sam wants his daughter. You want your dad. The real people, not imaginary ones. You've got to get used to each other. Now we'd better be moving. I don't want to have to find my way back in the dark. Dark in Africa is real dark."

Then

The sun was high by the time Greb's challenge ended, so the tribe rested in the shallows of the bay, re-forming their family groups, fussing over anyone who'd been hurt in the melee, unsure, and unhappy. The seniors visited Presh where he lay at the edge of the wave lap, conscious now, but with his eyes shut, and moaning at the slightest movement of his leg. Ma-ma and Hooa were with him, stroking his body beneath the water, and wetting his face often.

The visitors peered at him, muttering mournfully. The tribe needed a Leader, but not one with a broken leg. They grieved because they liked Presh, but also because they felt things wouldn't be right until a new Leader established himself. Meanwhile Presh's authority remained strong. When Ma-ma and Hooa tried to begin to tow him to calmer shallows at the end of the beach, he barked at them to stop and they obeyed.

There was a further worry. These shingle beaches swarmed at night with savage little crabs which scavenged for flesh, living or dead. They would pick a stranded fish, however large, down to its skeleton by morning. They would do the same with Presh. As the sun moved on and the tribe began to think about foraging again before the night, Ma-ma and Hooa became increasingly fretful, and when Tong visited he stayed, sharing their anxiety. He took Presh's arm as if to tow him elsewhere but then, like the females, obeyed the order to stop. Despairing, he looked around, saw Li close by, and grunted, *What to do?*

Li had been as worried as the others. Presh, she could see, must be moved. He must be towed at high tide, soon before dark, out to the headland and lifted onto a shelf just above the water, where he could spend the night. And then, tomorrow . . . But tomorrow was tomorrow. First, he had to be moved, and for that to happen his leg must be protected.

She could see it in the clear water, foot and ankle grossly swollen. She could sense the grind of the bone ends as the leg moved in the water. She must stop that grinding. When Greb had broken Nuhu's arm . . . What could she use? There was nothing in the slop and slither of the sea. She looked along the barren little beach. A curtain of creeper hung from the cliff. A ridge of dried tide wrack marked the highest reach of the waves. She left the water and climbed the burning shingle, thinking perhaps if she made a bundle of wrack and bound it around with creeper . . . A white gleam in the wrack caught her eye. Bone? She pulled the object free and found it was a crooked branch, wave worn and sun bleached. The thought of bone was still there, so she laid it against her leg. The bent part at the end followed the line of her feet. Something fizzed in her mind and said, *Yes. I can do it.*

Carrying the branch, she climbed and tested the creeper, swung herself up the mat, and bit through suitable strands, as she had done for earlier attempts at net making. On her way back to the water she gathered an armful of wrack and settled at the edge of the wave lap to experiment on her own leg. This was awkward. She turned, saw Tong watching from the water, and grunted *Come help.* Children never gave commands to adults, but he came without resentment, only puzzled that she wanted to do things to his leg when it was Presh's that needed her healing magic.

Her mind was still fizzing but her movements were slow. Her earlier experiments with creepers, reeds, and grasses had taught her that a step-by-step approach was best, trying out each element and testing its possibilities and limits before moving on. She laid the branch beside Tong's leg, looped creeper around it to hold it in place, padded it with wrack, and tied the creeper more firmly, making adjustments till she was happy. She untied the bundle and turned toward Presh.

He would have to be right out on the beach. She couldn't work in the water. Again she called *Come help,* and set Tong and Hooa by his shoulders and Ma-ma by his waist while she readied herself to look after the broken leg. Having seen her experimenting on Tong's leg, they now understood what she wanted, and as soon as she grunted a *Now* they bent and lifted Presh.

At once he barked *Stop.* They stopped and looked at Li. She gestured and grunted another *Now,* and again they lifted Presh, and this time merely hesitated at his bark and then carried on, though he wrestled to loose Tong's grip and cried with pain. As soon as he was out on the beach Ma-ma knelt by him, coaxing and soothing and stroking his mane. When Li started to work he tried to kick her away with his good leg, so that it took three males to hold him still. By now the helpers had understood what was

needed—it had been the means, the possibilities and diffi-
culties, that had been beyond them. Even Presh in the end
lay still, only wincing or moaning as his leg was moved to
work the lashings beneath it. By then many of the tribe
had returned to the headland to forage, and a shark watch
had been set, though at intervals they'd come back to see
what was happening and to help keep a cooling spatter of
water over the group on the beach. There was a return of
confidence and security. The tribe had its Leader, though
he was hurt for the time being. Li would see that he got
well.

When they'd finished they carried Presh down into the
water and towed him out toward the headland. He didn't
resist. It would be hard to say how much the splint Li had
made prevented the break from hurting, and how much
the change was due to the fact that once his commands
had been overruled to get him out of the water, both he
and the tribe accepted that that would happen again if he
tried to resist. Perhaps too his body and mind had become
used to the pain and he was more able to cope with it. At
any rate they took him out to where he could lie in a calm
inlet and food could be brought for him, and then as the
sun went down and the tide reached its full they lifted him
out onto a smooth flat rock to spend the night. Hooa
stayed with him for warmth and company while the others
climbed up to their regular roosting ledge to sleep.

By morning the sea had changed. Last night's near-calm
had become a slow heave of waves from the main ocean,
which as the tide rose slopped onto the rock where Presh
lay, the larger ones covering him and tugging at his body as
they retreated. The tribe understood these signs and knew
that by evening full-scale rollers would be dashing themselves in spume and thunder against the headland.

Li, exhausted, slept late. When she climbed down she found several of the adults bobbing in the water clear of the rock where Presh lay, watching him anxiously but not doing anything. He rose on one elbow to watch as she slid up beside him and tested the wrappings around his leg. The wrack had swollen with wetting and some of the vine strands had worked loose. Crouching to shield the leg from the waves with her body, Li refastened the lashings and signaled to the others to come and help Presh into the water, but at once he snorted disapproval and before anyone could stop him used the backwash of the next wave to ease himself to the lip of the ledge, and on the next slid deftly into the sea, letting Li lift the wrapped leg clear of the rock as he went.

The effort must have hurt but Presh refused to make pain noises as he let the others tow him clear of the rocks to rest in the lulling swell. Ma-ma and Hooa brought him food and the tribe spread out to forage as much as they could before the waves became dangerous. They felt that their world had returned almost to normal. They had their Leader, and though his leg was broken Li had worked her magic and it would soon mend.

Only Li was worried. She was thinking about fresh water, for Presh to drink. (Spending so much time in the sea, the tribe didn't yet have the human need to sweat, which demands pints of drinking water every day. Their main need was to wash the salts from their diet out of their bodies from time to time, and they could go several days together without a drink, but then it became essential. Their whole economy depended on moving up and down the coast, balancing out their needs for food and drink and shelter.)

During the rains fresh water streamed for a few days out of the sky, runneled down cliffs and filled every hollow, but for the rest of the year there were only three places. There was the river at the northern edge of their territory; the bay with the water caves where they'd trapped the shark, which they had left only the day before Presh had fought with Greb; and a place three days further south where a steady flow of fresh water welled up from the sea bed, enough in calm weather to make a wide pool where you felt your buoyancy lessen as you swam into it.

In none of these places was there enough food, and only at the bay was there shelter. The river held muddy fish and clams, but also crocodiles. From trees on the bank fell a fruit whose fermenting juices made you dance and shout and rollick for a while, and then fall sad, but there were leopards and other night hunters so the tribe would arrive at the river on a morning around new moon, post lookouts landward and seaward, and leave before dark on their tide-like drift down the coast.

At the bay there was food for two days, at most, for the whole tribe, while along the glaring coral beaches behind the sea pool there was none at all. Still it was a place of great happiness. They took care to feed well before they reached it and would arrive with shouts of joy, and splash for a while across and around the pool and then, without any signal, form a rough ring and dive one after the other to the place where the water streamed out and allow it to take them back to the surface, soaring like gulls in an up-draft. There were no fights there, and kin quarrels were forgotten. The children chased through the frothing shallows while the adults lolled in deeper water, greeting each other as they went to and from the pool to drink, and couples who were ready swam a little way apart and mated. If they'd had words for such a thought, they'd have called the pool holy. They came there twice a month for the middle part of a day, going south toward the shrimping grounds or back again north, moving as the moon changed, as both they and the moon seemed to have done forever. Now the thought of their next visit to the pool was already growing in their minds.

It was in Li's mind too, but how could Presh make that journey? Between feeding places the tribe moved steadily, close inshore where possible, wary of sharks. Towing Presh would slow them and make them more vulnerable, and would need a calm sea, which they were soon not going to have. How would his leg mend, constantly in movement in the water? Where would he sleep? There were only two sets of caves on the coast, and elsewhere the tribe used ledges with a difficult climb to them, which no predator would make.

No, he must lie on land, in shade, with drinking water easy. There was only one place, the bay with the water caves. He must go back.

Li swam off to look for Tong who was family-close and had been her main helper the night before, but found him in confrontation with Kerif. With Presh unable to patrol the tribe and remind everyone of his authority, it was natural for the other males to start jostling for status, so Tong and Kerif were face-to-face beyond the headland, rising and falling, yelling their challenges and sluicing their arches of water. It was still more like a game than a serious contest for leadership, but their minds were filled with it. Nor could Li have brought herself to interrupt. Though she was aware of her own new status in the tribe, she knew that it only worked some of the time. Now, with two adult males engaged in something that took all their energies and attention, she was an unnoticed child. Li watched for a while but the contest showed no sign of ending, so she swam back to Presh.

He too was anxious, but only about his need to move on

from this exposed headland. "On" for him meant south, past more headlands with shingle beaches between, plagued by the savage crabs, and eventually to the coral beaches and the fresh-water pool. He had not considered how long it would take to get him there, where he would sleep, how great his need to drink would become. Normally before a move he'd have gone around the scattered families expressing his restlessness in sounds and signals, making them feel restless also, so that when he at last swam off they'd all have been ready to go. But it was different here. There was still plenty of food and it was important to eat all they could before the sea rose. No one expected to move or wanted to. Even Ma-ma and Hooa, who'd been attending to Presh's needs and could sense his anxiety, could only mutter soothingly to him and coax him to stay where he was.

He was relieved to see Li, but astonished and angry when she grunted a *Come help* to Hooa, put an arm under his arm, and started to tow him north. Her idea was to take him to Tong and Kerif and use his authority to stop their contest. Then, somehow, she would have to get him to detach Tong and a few of the others to help tow him back to the water caves while the rest of the tribe continued their usual journey south. They couldn't all go back. They'd just stripped that section almost bare of food. So it would have to be like that.

At one level Li was aware that she was asking something almost impossible. You simply didn't leave the tribe. To do so was a kind of dying. The tribe was where you belonged. But the need was now so obvious to her that at her surface level she couldn't see that the others would be unable to grasp it.

So Presh resisted and Ma-ma and Hooa didn't know what to do but at length gave in to Li's insistence. They found Tong and Kerif, their contest over, feeding together, touching each other often, and sharing any prey they caught. They peered briefly at Presh, grunted commiseration, and returned to the vital business of remaking their friendship.

It was the same with all the others. They were hungry and occupied with settling into themselves after yesterday's upheaval. They didn't want to move. Only two attached themselves to Li's group, a young male, Goor, who was in the stage of splitting himself off from his immediate family, and the stranger whose baby had died, Rawi—Presh had always been kind to her and she would have liked to mate with him.

Presh was too tired, too shaken by his loss of command to resist anymore. Ma-ma and Hooa were deeply worried about leaving the tribe and at first gave signs of wanting to break off and return, but then became afraid to leave the little group. Rawi and Goor were readier for the idea and did most of the work, towing Presh through the rising swell, lying on their backs and kicking with their webbed feet, the tribe's usual stroke for longer journeys.

Normally it would have taken them less than half a day to reach the caves from that headland, but it was almost dark when they came to the bay, hungry and exhausted, and working together lifted the unconscious Presh across the rocky foreshore and into the smaller cave.

Now:
Tuesday Morning

Vinny woke with the sun shining into her eyes and remembered where she was. They'd finished putting the tent up in the dark, but now when she looked around she saw that it was as large as a small room, with her cot on one side and Dad's on the other and plenty of space between. There were mosquito nets at each end to let the wind blow through. Dad's cot was empty.

She twisted out of bed, tapped out her slippers, and still in her pajamas pushed out through the netting. The dawn air smelled as it had yesterday only more so, with fewer human smells to muddle it. In front of her, shadow-streaked in the sunrise, rose the outcrop. Dad was already up there, digging. She could see his yellow shirt bent beside the big rock.

He'd left a note for her on the folding table. "Breakfast at site, please. Banana, coffee, muesli, two slices bread, and Marmite." She put the kettle onto the propane burner, dressed, got two breakfasts ready, put everything carefully back into its

containers the way he'd shown her and carried the food
bag up the slope.

By the time she reached him Dad had taken his shirt off
and was streaming with sweat, so that all his tanned skin
glistened and the muscles showed clear. Vinny had seen
him half stripped yesterday, but hadn't realized then how
fit and strong he must be, certainly compared with Colin
who had a bit of a beer belly and regarded watching American football on TV as good exercise.

"'Morning," he said. "Sleep well?"

"Oh, yes. I found your note. I think I've got it right.
How much hotter is it going to get?"

"Same as yesterday, give or take the odd degree. There
comes a point where you don't notice the variations. Beats
me why our ancestors chose to evolve in a moderate
oven."

"It was the other way around. They found themselves in
the oven so they went into the sea to get out of it and then
they evolved."

He was unscrewing the thermos as she spoke and didn't
pause. In spite of May Anna's encouragement Vinny
hadn't meant to barge straight in like that, but she'd been
thinking about the coming heat, and how lovely it would
be to have sea to swim in, while she'd been bringing the
food bag up the hill.

"I don't follow the logic of it," he said mildly.

"They'd need to stand up to keep their heads out of the
water," said Vinny. "And the water would help too. I
mean, if chimps started wanting to hunt or something on
their hind legs, they'd have a terrible time. They'd actually
be slower than they are now. And all their bits would be in
the wrong place. And they'd get frightful backaches—we
still do. And—you know—sinuses—they don't drain right

because of the way we've got to hold our heads now . . ."

"That argument would apply however our ancestors learned to walk upright. So would many of the others."

"That's not the point, Dad. The point is there'd have to have been something which made it worthwhile—I mean which actually made it easy, like having water to hold you up while you were learning to stand. And of course they wouldn't need fur . . ."

"Otters have fur. So do some seals."

"But most of them don't, and whales and dolphins don't. But they have fat under their skins like us . . ."

"Elephants are pretty well hairless. Are you going to tell me . . . ?"

"Elaine Morgan says elephants have webbed feet. She thinks they might have been water animals once. Their trunks are sort of snorkels. I can't remember about the fat."

"You expect me to take this seriously?"

"I just want to know. I mean, the idea about elephants seems weird, okay. But a lot of animals are weird, Dad. *We're* weird. We just think we're normal. If you could get the other animals to tell us what they thought, I bet they'd say we're weirder than any of them."

He gave her an unreadable look and fell into one of his silences. She watched him cut his Marmite sandwich into exact triangles, just the way she herself would have done. I'm his daughter too, she thought. I may look like Mom. Some of those old photos of Mom that Granny's got, you wouldn't know it wasn't me, but if Dad wants to be silent, I can show him I'm happy with that too. That's not pretending.

So she ate, and watched the shadows change across the puckered badlands and thought about when it had been marsh, drying out, and the sea had been right over there, beyond those hills, until he stretched and put his mug down and looked at her and nodded.

"Better get on," he said.

"Can I see what you've been doing?"

"Just shifting dirt so far. I'll do a bit more and then we'll rig the awning and we'll get down to something more interesting."

He'd done a lot since Vinny had last seen the site. The miniquarry she and Dr. Hamiska had made had become a trench wide enough to work in, running several feet into the hill. Its floor sloped upward, though far less steeply than the hill. That must be how the underlying strata lay. All that was left of the quarry was an eight-inch step at the entrance to the trench, because so far Dad had been cutting in just above the layers with the fossils in them. She could see the darker line of tuff at the bottom of the step. The floor of the quarry had changed.

"Where's my bone?" she said.

"Your bone?"

"It was there. I was digging it out and Joe came to see and dug some more and that's when he found the toe bone. I wanted to try and draw it. It was a bit of shoulder blade, he said."

"Oh, that. It was in the way so I took it out. It'll be in one of the bags . . . Here . . . don't lose the label."

It took Vinny a while to find a way of propping her parasol to give her enough shade to work in. By then Dad was slogging away at the back of the trench, hacking the earth out with a pick, shoveling it into two buckets and carrying it to his spoil heap down the hill. The further he went in, of course, the more earth he had to move to get down to the fossil layers.

The label had figures on it which meant nothing to

Vinny. The fossil, now that she could see the whole thing, turned out smaller than she'd expected, a thin flat triangle, broken along two sides and with a hole near one corner. Another corner was cracked off, but the pieces fitted neatly together. The longest side was a bit more than three inches. She turned the larger piece over and over in her hands, trying to look at it the way Nikki said you had to, as though it were the only thing in the world. Then she settled down to try and draw it.

Mrs. Clulow, who taught art at St. Brigid's, used to tell Vinny to try and "free up," whatever that meant, but in the end she'd given in and let her draw and paint her own way, with every line as exact as she could make it. Vinny thought Dürer's engraving of a hare—she kept a Christmas card of it pinned over her bed—was the most beautiful picture she knew. Dürer would have been good at fossils. She worked steadily, locked in a cell which contained only her and the bone and her pad and pencil. She used a 4H to make faint lines, which she rubbed out again and again until she was satisfied. She realized how much time had passed only when the shadow of her parasol left the edge of her pad.

Dad was straightening from his trench and must have seen her shift position.

"How are you doing?" he said.

"Okay. It's easier being flat. Round would be much more difficult."

"Mind if I look?"

Vinny passed the pad across. She didn't want to feel he was judging her.

"Do you know what it is?" she said. "A pig or something?"

"Very difficult with something so broken. I'd have said it was too big for a pig. Or a hominid, of course."

"A hippo?"

"Um. I don't think so. I haven't seen that many hippo scapulae. It's the sort of thing you'd need a specialist to identify, and even then . . . What are these lines here? Shading?"

"No. At least, well, I think they're there, only sometimes I can't see them. Like the man in the moon, sort of."

"Let's have a look at the bone."

Surprised, she passed it across. He peered, wiped sweat from his eyes, peered again and fetched a magnifying glass from his satchel and studied the bone through it, turning it to vary the angle of light. The lines he'd asked about were faint curves, like parts of several exact circles, close together around the hole.

"Yes, they're there all right," he said.

"Do they mean something?"

"Hard to say. If we'd found them somewhere else, say on a known neolithic site with stone tools around, or animal bones with butchery incisions, the natural interpretation would be that the hole had been deliberately bored with a pointed stone flake. That doesn't make sense here."

"Why not?"

"Because whatever the date of this site is, however you interpret Fred's pig data and the geological sequences, we're still at least a couple of million years too early. Right, are you ready to give me a hand?"

"Oh, yes, please."

By now it was starting to get really hot, so they rigged the awning to shade the trench and Vinny lashed her parasol to one of the poles to make an extra patch of shade. Then Dad started to work his way along the floor of the trench, down into the fossil layers. He'd removed the precious toe bone last night and May Anna had taken it back to the camp. Now he probed delicately with his trowel tip into the soil, loosened a morsel, and crumbled it between his fingers into a bucket. When he'd cleared a patch about half an inch deep and a few inches square he brushed the loose bits into the bucket and moved on until he'd worked about a foot along the trench and all the way across. Vinny took the bucket down the hill and tipped it onto a plastic sheet, separate from the main spoil heap. Later someone would sieve it through in case Dad had missed a tiny chip. Meanwhile Dad started to go down another half inch.

There was nothing in the first two layers, but on the next Dad said, "Let's have the steel rule. Thanks. Got a label? 13.5, 26.1, 11.8. Now the dental pick. Thanks."

He pecked delicately at what looked like a scrap of seashell, got it loose, and handed it out. Vinny put it into a bag and attached the label. Deliberately she didn't ask what it was—he'd tell her if he wanted to. There were more bits of shell in the next layer, which he photographed in place and told her to put into a single bag, and more still in the next, with what looked like the tail of a lizard projecting from the wall of the trench. Dad painted it with hardening fluid and was cutting around it when Vinny heard the growl of an engine as the driver changed gear to cross the dry riverbed.

"Someone's coming," she said.

"Joe," said Dad. "We're lucky to have had this long."

He went on working. A few minutes later the truck appeared, nosing its way through the hummocks and scrub below the outcrop. It stopped and several people climbed out. Dr. Hamiska pointed and gave instructions, and the others started to unload while he came striding up the slope with Dr. Wessler trailing behind him.

Dad had stopped work to watch him come.

"By the way," he muttered. "Don't show anyone your sketch for the moment, and don't say anything about those marks on the scapula. I'm not trying to hide anything, but I can do without a lot of crazy unsubstantiated theorizing till we've got a bit more to go on."

As soon as he was in earshot Dr. Hamiska stopped and flung up an arm as if he were posing for a war memorial.

" 'I can call spirits from the vasty deep,' " he cried.

"I'll settle for a cold lager," said Dad.

Dr. Hamiska loosed his great laugh, strode on, and peered in under the awning.

"Terrific, Sam," he said. "You must have been sweating your guts out. Found anything new?"

"Nothing much. Some shell-fragments. That lizard there. I'm getting on fairly fast now I've got the spoil cleared. The layer above the tuff seems to be only about twenty centimeters deep."

"The land was rising. The lake would have dried out."

"Possibly. What was that about spirits?"

"I put a call through to Craig. I wanted Amanda to know her trip out here wouldn't be wasted."

Dr. Hamiska glanced at Dad to see how he'd take it. Dad stiffened.

"You told Amanda what we'd found," he said flatly.

"Naturally. She has a right to know."

"You want the world's press flooding out here?"

"Who said anything about the world's press?"

"Amanda will have been onto the agencies within ten minutes of getting your call."

"Oh, Sam, Sam. You suppose I didn't tell her not to spoil Craig's big day with a premature announcement. I'm not telling the media anything till I've got a whole skeleton to show them."

"Supposing it's there."

"Of course it's there. But meanwhile I've got to strengthen Amanda's hand so that she's in a position to fight her corner for funds inside Craig. And that's just what I've done. She called me back. She's still coming Thursday, of course, but now she's bringing John Wishart with her!"

Dad looked at him and sighed, as if it was the worst news he'd heard for months. Dr. Hamiska responded with another bellow of laughter. Baffled, Vinny looked at Dr. Wessler, who was standing beside her, smiling thin-lipped, like a spectator enjoying a sour sort of comedy.

"Dynamic Dr. Amanda Hutt," he said, "is the recently appointed head of the paleontology department at Craig Museum. John Jedediah Wishart, Junior, is the museum director, the big cheese."

"The absolute Gorgonzola," cried Dr. Hamiska. "So you see, Vinny, it's up to you now. You must work your magic for us again."

Not wanting to make things worse for Dad, Vinny managed to smile.

"I'll do my best," she said.

"Of course you will. I'm relying on you. What shall we have? A tibia, do you think, Fred?"

"How about an artifact?" said Dr. Wessler, joining in the teasing of Dad.

"Oh, yes! Vinny, would you please see that, in addition to a further selection of hominid bones, your father unearths a primitive but unarguable example of a stone tool."

Then

It was like living in a dream, alone at the water caves, just the six of them and the baby, no clamor, no quarrels, no scurry, no press of bodies to lie down among at night, no song to wake to in the morning. The rhythms of their normal life were so strong in them that as the moon reached full they woke at midnight and all except Presh went down into the high tide to hunt for shrimp, though there were none here. They returned and huddled in the cave, mourning their loneliness and the emptiness of stomachs used to being crammed at this hour.

They'd piled a bed of seaweed for Presh near the mouth of the cave, where the rising sun struck in to warm him as the day began but climbed out of sight before its heat grew too much to bear. Most days Li would untie the bundle around his leg and she and the other females would inspect the swollen limb, and stroke it for a while, and then Li would fasten the bundle again. As she became more skilled she was able to reduce the padding. The swelling subsided, and soon Presh could hunker himself about without much pain, and lie in the water during the heat of the day. Till then the females brought water in their cupped webbed hands to wet him, as they'd have done with a sick baby.

It was always poor foraging in the bay, and worse so soon after the tribe had passed through, so they foraged in turn along the outer shore. Hooa, bewildered by the change, was inseparable from Ma-ma, and Rawi usually went with them, so Li foraged with Goor. At first Goor had been almost as bewildered as Hooa, but realizing that he was the only healthy male in the party had given him confidence, especially when he was away from Presh's commanding presence. Unlike some males he was generous in sharing the food he found, and not too old, after feeding, for catch-as-catch-can and diving games along the rocks.

Li was poised twenty feet above clear water when she saw the dolphins. She hadn't expected them here. In her mind they belonged with the other bay, but now five of them were coming toward her in formation, surging out of the water with arched backs and then plunging under. She dived, crying *Follow* to Goor as she fell, and raced to meet them.

Before she'd dived she had seen the spattered surface in front of them, where the shoal they were hunting broke through in panic flight. By the time she was nearing them Goor had caught her up, and the shoal must have seen the two bodies in the water as two more hunters ahead. It swung aside, now heading directly for the bay. Where the rock spit loomed it might have turned again, but the leading fish saw the single channel of clear water ahead and took it, and the rest of the shoal, bound into formation by instinct, swirled through behind them.

The dolphins were unable to follow, but Li and Goor, racing along behind them and now wild with the thrill of the hunt, splashed across the bar and harried the shoal around the bay, yelling *Come help* to the others. Goor actually managed to grab a fish and fling it out onto the rocks, and Rawi caught another, but the rest of them had no luck and simply rushed and yelled and splashed, keeping the fish in a state of panic until the leaders found the entrance of the bay and headed through.

The dolphins were waiting for them. Deliberately, as if they were used to this way of hunting, they raced past the shoal, turned it, and headed it back toward the bay. Li and the others, gasping at the entrance, saw the catspaw ruffle in the water racing toward them and waited ready. As the shoal rushed through, packed by the narrows into an almost solid mass, they were able to snatch fish after fish and fling them over their shoulders to flounder on the rocks. Then they plunged into the bay, and knowing now what they were doing, harried their prey around along the shore and out again into the open sea where the dolphins waited.

Twice more the cycle was repeated before the remains of the shoal escaped, scurrying along below the southern crags. As Li stood panting on the rock spit two of the dolphins came cruising through the clear water beside her. All around her lay dead and dying fish. She picked a couple up and flung them out, and the dolphins rose and took them just as they hit the surface. Almost at once the other dolphins arrived and hung below her, waiting expectantly. Ma-ma, Hooa, and Rawi were already harvesting the fish on the other side of the entrance. Goor was carrying one up for Presh. The ones this side, Li felt, were rightly the dolphins' share.

When she had all but cleared the rocks around her she picked up the last two, slid down into the water, and kicked gently toward the dolphins. They backed away, so she waited, treading water, with a fish held in each hand until they became inquisitive and drifted in. Two of them took the fish, but suddenly they backed away again.

Goor had appeared beside her. She made a *Be still* sign and then they waited, rising to the surface only when they needed air. Li knew the dolphins were still nearby, because of the sounds they made, their wailing whistles and clicks, call and answer, filling the sea around her. Shadowy shapes loomed, neared, took shape, came close, circled until she could stroke the long flanks as they passed, and returned to caress themselves against her body.

Then they swam together, dolphins and people, through the greeny-golden sea world, not in a wild dance full of rush and foam but in a slow, close, gentle weaving of bodies in the friendly water, while the dolphins' song went on and on, filling the sea like the wavering sunlight. Li understood it to be song because the only sound she knew at all like it was the song of the tribe waking in the morning to greet the returning day.

The dolphins left without a signal, but the song continued in the water, dwindling as they went, until they rounded a headland and it was lost. Li and Goor waited a long while, hoping, but they didn't come back.

Gulls had gathered screaming for a share of the fish, but Ma-ma, Hooa, and Rawi had by now carried almost all that was left to the back of the cave, where it was cooler and the meat might last a little longer before it stank (though the tribe had strong stomachs, and needed them). Li took one to eat and rested in the blood-warm shallows. Thoughts drifted through her mind—the hunt, the dance, the song. These things had a meaning, a pattern she could almost see. It didn't cross her mind that it might be part of the dolphins' hunting technique to harry a shoal toward the shore and pen them in some inlet to catch them there, and that they'd never meant to chase this one into the bay,

where they couldn't get at it. If there hadn't been helpers
in the bay to force the shoal back again they'd have had a
poor hunt. To her it was obvious that the dolphins had
come because she needed them, because she was hungry
and they were her friends. They were so much wiser than
she was. They knew where the sun was born.

A few days later the dolphins came again, nine or ten of
them and herding a large shoal. Goor saw them first and
called *Come help.* The others were racing to the bar when
the shoal swept through on a wave surge. They chased it
out, and this time, as the tide was lower than before and
the water at the bar shallower, the fish had to thresh across
in a packed mass, where they were almost as easy to pick
out as anchored mussels. The dolphins drove them in
again, but were less lucky with the wave and half the shoal
jibbed at the bar and broke free. Next time the rest escaped, but by then the shelving rocks beside the bar were
covered with silver bodies, and Li and Goor could fling
plenty out to the cruising dolphins, leaving masses still to
be carried back to the cave. The dolphins didn't stay, but
as soon as they'd fed enough flipped on their sides and
swam off.

That evening in babble and clamor the tribe arrived.
They were hungry. Tong and Kerif were still disputing the
leadership, with three other males joining in temporary
alliances which stopped anything from being settled. The
tribe's journey to the shrimping beach and back had been
governed not by whether they'd stripped all they could
from a feeding ground but by one of the contenders trying
to enhance his prestige by getting the tribe to move against
the other's will. So the tribe had come to the shrimping
beach in separate groups and found poor harvesting there,
with the sea not calm and the high tide less than usual. By

the time they reached the bay with the water caves their stomachs were rumbling with hunger.

It was Kerif's fault, and Tong's. When times were good Leaders accepted the prestige, but when times were bad the blame was all on them. It was in this mood that the tribe streamed into the bay and saw Presh sitting by a cave mouth in the evening shadow, chewing the back muscles out of succulent fish.

He rose, supporting himself against the rock but managing to look as if he had expected their return. His leg was still too weak to bear his weight, but Li had decided only that morning that it would be safe to take the splint off. The bone had set crooked above the ankle, and the calf muscles were shrunken, but otherwise Presh was in fine fettle. He had eaten well, drunk fresh water, rested in the healing sea, been cosseted by females, and slept untroubled in the cave. His muscles moved easily under the blue-black skin and his mane was glossy with health.

The tribe had half forgotten, during the separation, that Presh existed, but now they remembered and scampered up the rocks with cries of greeting. They fawned on him, inspected his leg, and wheedled for his fish. At this point Hooa came out of the cave with a fish of her own and stood in baffled happiness, staring at the newcomers. Presh took her fish and passed it to Kerif with a lordly *I give,* and the same for Tong with the one he'd been eating. He barked *Fetch* to Hooa, meaning her to get him another one, but by then the tribe, eager for fresh water, were pressing into the caves, jostling to reach the thin, sweet trickles down the rocks.

They found the fish by smell in the dark and squabbled over them till they realized that there were enough for even the weakest to get a share, so they finished the day feasting on the spits by the mouth of the bay, where the rocks still held the warmth of the sun. It was obvious to all of them that Presh had arranged this feast as a reward for their return to his unquestionable leadership. He accepted their fawnings and touchings with great good humor. His prestige was immense.

Prestige is like food. It must be frequently given and taken or its effect dwindles away. A full stomach will see people through a day and a night, and maybe another day, but by the second evening they'll be hungry again. Prestige lasts longer, but not very long among people with empty stomachs. Next morning Li came as usual to inspect Presh's leg, to stroke and feel it and wonder what might be happening to the bone inside. She felt ill at ease. Alone with her small group life had seemed straightforward. Presh had been Leader, but he was hurt, so he and the others had simply accepted that Li knew what should be done. And when they were hungry she would arrange for the dolphins to bring them fish.

The tribe knew nothing of that. They had almost forgotten that Li might be in some way different. She was a child like other children, to be ignored unless she got in their way. Not that she wanted prestige for herself, but she was no longer certain how she fitted in, and that made her anxious.

Tong came to pay his morning respects. Presh should have risen, allowing Tong to dip his own head and shoulders as a signal of acceptance of Presh's superiority, but Presh stayed seated, looking lordly and confident. Puzzled, Tong peered into his eyes, then remembered about the leg and bent to inspect it. Presh had already tried it out and realized from the pain that it wouldn't yet bear his weight, but he didn't wish to have to hunker ignobly down to the sea in front of the whole tribe. Now he seized his chance. As Tong rose Presh put his arm around his shoulder and used him to help himself to his feet. His free hand grabbed Li's shoulder. Between them he hobbled down to the water, demonstrating that even a senior male must do what he, Presh, wanted.

Once in the sea he was mobile enough, paddling with his hands and kicking with his good leg. He visited the families as usual, and set a shark watch so that the tribe could scatter along the outer shore to forage. There was never a lot of food there, but they'd fed well the previous night and didn't complain.

Next day, though, stomachs were empty. People had drunk the fresh water they needed and the shore was picked bare. It was time to move, but the next good feeding ground was a long swim north and included a land trip across the neck of a headland whose sheer cliffs gave swimmers nowhere to climb to if sharks were sighted. Presh knew his leg wasn't yet up to it and gave no signal for a move. By noon the tribe were restless and by evening they were angry. If there'd been a single alternative Leader he'd have taken the chance to confront Presh, who'd have had no answer, and the tribe would have started north whether he wanted to or not. Tong and Kerif began a series of challenge and counterchallenge, but night came before they could settle the matter one way or the other.

Li slept badly. Her anxiety had increased with the tension in the tribe. She felt herself to be bound to Presh, as Leader, by ties like those which bound her to Ma-ma. To the others in the tribe his weakness, and Kerif's confrontation with Tong, and the almost inevitable change of leadership, were simply events to be accepted as they accepted most things within their experience, like a poor tide at the shrimping beach, something beyond their power to alter. But Li, just as she had at the shark hunt, could see what needed to be done. The one possible solution was clear in her mind. The dolphins must bring another shoal of fish.

She lay in the dark, calling to them in her mind, silent *Come here*s and *Help*s. And then, still thinking these calls, she tried to make them in the way the dolphins would understand, their own calls which she'd heard when she danced with them in the water. In silence she remade their song—the long wailings that died and recovered and wavered, and the clicks, and the pauses which were like the ghosts of sounds. She filled her inward dark with the song of the dolphins until the cave around her seemed to whisper it aloud. She cried to them for help. Without words she prayed to them.

No answer came, but at first light she swam to the bar and peered through the dazzle of the rising sun for dark backs arching from the sea. She lowered herself into the water and listened, but heard only the slap and slither of ripple on rock. She climbed up to stare out to sea, saw nothing, and dipped again below to listen for the first whisper of the song.

So in, so out, as the sun climbed. Tong and Kerif were starting their struggle in the bay, but she didn't look around, only glancing at times to check that Presh was still nearby, lolling in the water and pretending not to have noticed the confrontation, though if he'd had his full strength he'd long ago have intervened to suppress such impertinence.

She heard them first, but waited till she was sure that the sound was coming nearer. Then she climbed and stood tiptoe on the rocks, gazing east. Dark flecks rose from the long slope of a wave. She turned, plunged into the bay, and swam to Presh and tugged at his arm, calling *Come*. He stared at her. For a child, even Li, to try to command the Leader . . . *Come,* she called, and tugged harder; and now, knowing his need of her, he allowed himself to be persuaded up onto the rocks where he sat and looked along the line of her pointing arm.

The dolphins were nearing now, spread into their hunting formation. The driven shoal puckered the water before them. Presh knew these signs—he'd seen two hunts from the cave mouth. He grabbed Li's shoulder, almost forcing her to her knees as he hauled himself up to stand on his good leg. He bellowed to the tribe over his shoulder. A few heads turned, but before anyone had time to react the forerunners of the shoal came streaming over the bar.

Only Rawi, who was always hanging around somewhere near Presh, both understood what was happening and had time to get to the bar and grab a couple of fish, and then the whole shoal had swept through and the bay was full of people trying to catch them, keeping them at the pitch of panic, breaking the shoal into scattered groups which rushed to and fro until a group found the gap again and headed out. By then Presh, still using Li for support, bellowing and gesturing to force his authority through the tumult, had organized a dozen adults to be waiting ready in the shallows.

They found it easy hunting. The whole tribe saw the silver bodies arcing through the air to flop onto the rocks. Now that they understood what was needed they spread out across the bay, rounded up the rest of the shoal, and drove it all together to the entrance, where it met the earlier group which the waiting dolphins had already headed back. The shallows frothed with fish and people. Fish streamed through the air. The cliffs echoed with hunt yells.

There was a pause while the shoal broke free until the dolphins rounded them up and headed them back again, and Presh took the chance to organize a ring of people inside the bar, others poised on the rocks ready to grab the

harvest from the shallows, and yet others to dive in outside
and help the dolphins bar the escape. The shoal came. He
bellowed for action. The tribe screamed. The water all
around the bar was white foam and shining dark bodies,
people and dolphins together, while the children rushed
squealing around the rocks, dodging the hail of fish.

Then it was over, and the rocks were silvered with shining bodies. The haul was immense, beyond experience.
Presh stood punching the air with his free hand, bellowing
and triumphing, lord of the hunt, until Li managed to
attract his attention. His first thought was to lift her high to
share in the triumph, but as soon as he let go of her shoulder he staggered and half fell. She helped him down, and
when he tried to rise again she backed away and called
Come, and pointed seaward. He looked puzzled. She
picked up a fish and threw it to a passing dolphin. *Come
help,* she called.

Now he understood and hunkered across, picking up a
fish as he came. A dolphin came cruising through the clear
water and he tossed the fish to it, then laughed with triumph as it rose and took the gift. Kerif was standing close
by, chewing meat he'd bitten from the fish in his hand.
Presh gestured to him and barked *Do it,* but Kerif stood
baffled till another dolphin swam by and Presh barked and
gestured again. Reluctantly Kerif threw the fish to it, but
his feelings seemed to change as the dolphin rose and took
it, and he too laughed and spread his arms wide and
punched the air.

These signals made sense. Though the people often
squabbled over small prey, when a hunter found something
large enough to be shared he increased his prestige by dol-
ing out bits of it to allies and rivals. This was a vital part of
the pattern of gestures and calls which kept the tribe whole
and orderly, understanding each other's needs, helping

each other survive. Now the other seniors lined the rock to give back a proper share of this immense treasure of food, and the dolphins thronged below to take it. Li watched for a while, laughing and triumphing with the others. Then she took Presh by the arm and persuaded him down into the water and out to wait until the dolphins had had their fill, making signs to him to keep still when she saw them turning from the rock.

They came nosing past, close enough for her to stroke a flank, and she thought that was all, but they wheeled and returned and the dance began.

Presh didn't try to swim with them, but stayed still and became a fixed point in the dolphins' to-and-fro weavings, letting them slide past him with long, caressing movements while the broken sunlight rippled off their backs and the sea was full of their song. The tribe were in the water now, shadowy watchers, but when some of the males swam nearer Presh gestured *Go away,* and they retreated, obedient as children. Still he didn't question Li's right to be there, joining as best she could in the pattern the dolphins made and sharing as she did so in his glory. He knew what she had done. He was a wise leader. While Kerif and Tong had been confronting each other in the bay and he'd been pretending not to notice, he had all the time been aware of Li, out on the rocks, waiting, staring seaward. The triumph was his, indisputable, but he knew it was Li who had caused it to happen. She was the one who could call the dolphins.

Now:
Tuesday
Afternoon

By lunchtime there was a large awning erected at
the bottom of the hill, and a little one a few yards
along from where Dad was working, to shade a
second trench. By now it was too hot for work out
in the open, so after lunch everyone rested. Dad
made Vinny go and lie down while he wrote up his
notes. She'd never have believed she could sleep in
that heat, but she did, for nearly two hours. When
she woke it was still roastingly hot, but she looked
out of the tent and saw that the others were up on
the hill again, so she climbed slowly up to see if she
could still help. The moment she arrived she realized that Dad was in a bad mood, deep in one of his
silences. It didn't take her long to find out why.

Dr. Wessler had (typically, Vinny guessed) got
out of doing the heavy preliminary work of open-
ing up the second trench, and he and the Hamiskas
and anyone else who could be spared were spread
out surveying the rest of the outcrop for possible
further sites. Meanwhile Watson Azikwe and Michael Haddu were hacking out the soil above the
fossil layer and carting it down to the tip. They

were both Africans. Michael was a grizzled, roly-poly man who (Dad had told her) had left school when he was twelve. He'd been on a lot of expeditions like this in other countries, starting as a laborer but becoming interested, so that by now he knew more about fieldwork than a lot of highly qualified experts.

Watson was Dr. Azikwe, but Vinny couldn't think of him like that. He was quite young, for one thing, only twenty-something. He wore three gold chains under a gaudy open shirt. Vinny thought he was fun. She enjoyed his style, and the way he assumed that all the world was going to like him as much as he liked himself. The trouble was, Dad didn't.

It was Watson's fault. While Michael was hacking out a fresh barrow load of spoil, Watson squatted by Dad's trench, chattering away about his time in Europe and America, and the well-known paleontologists he'd met. Dad was crouched out of sight. Vinny heard one or two grunts—snorts, more like, to Vinny's ears—but Watson treated them as encouragement to keep the conversation going. It wasn't that Watson was shirking. As soon as Michael called to him he gangled himself up and wheeled the full barrow down the slope. Dad straightened in the trench, wiped his face with his shirt, and took a swig of water from his bottle.

"I've had about as much of that chap as I can stand," he muttered.

"Poor Dad. Do you want me to try and distract him?"

"It would be like trying to distract the Victoria Falls."

"I'll ask him to explain about something."

"Why not? Try him on these—he says he's done some work on mollusks, and he seems to know his stuff, in spite of everything. Keep them with the H-layer material—that bag there."

He passed out his latest collection of shell fragments. Vinny lashed her parasol to an awning pole and laid out the pieces in its shade. By now Watson was doing his stint with the pick and shovel while Michael rested, so she had a bit of time. Most of the pieces were from something like a mussel, about the size of her thumb joint, but there were three from a creature which must have been about as big as her palm. The H-layer was important—it was the one which had had the hominid fossils in it, immediately above the tuff. She sorted through the bag and found several more pieces of larger shell.

Watson straightened from his work, sweating. Michael rose and took the barrow. Watson took a few more thumps with the pick, but as there was nowhere to shovel the spoil to now he laid it aside and climbed out of the trench. Vinny looked innocently up.

"Do you know what these are, Watson?"

Affably he crouched beside her.

"Bivalves, you know," he said. "Some kind of Tridacna, this one."

"What about this big one? I thought I'd try and fit the bits together."

He picked up the largest piece and turned it over.

"Don't know for sure," he said. "Mytilacea, maybe. Take a lot of comparison, lot of studying, be sure of something like that."

"Can you tell if it was freshwater or if it came out of the sea? It would be terrific if it came out of the sea. Do you know about Elaine Morgan's sea-ape theory?"

Watson laughed, macho contemptuous.

"That woman," he said. "Hey! Sam! What you been telling your daughter?"

Dad hadn't heard, or was pretending he hadn't. Vinny knew she'd made a bad mistake. If Watson started teasing

him in front of the others about his daughter's wild ideas,
he'd clam up completely. Dr. Hamiska would probably
join in. She was with one part of her mind aware that she
ought to try and repair the damage, change the subject, or
laugh at herself and her own silly ideas, but another part of
her mind refused to let her. It mattered, in ways she didn't
understand, that she shouldn't pretend about this,
shouldn't play the part of an ignorant little girl who
couldn't think for herself. May Anna said the ideas might
be wrong, but they weren't crazy. Vinny was certain she
knew more about them than Watson did. Her reaction
now was to get angry, the way Mom would have when
something like this happened.

"What do you mean, that woman?" she snapped.
"What difference does it make she's a woman? I bet you
haven't even read her book. You tell me why you've got a
layer of fat under your skin, like sea mammals, and fur like
an otter's when you were in your mother's womb, and a
rotten sense of smell, and a lot of people have webbed
fingers and toes, and all sorts of things land animals don't
need. Go on. Tell me. Don't bother Dad about it. Tell
me!"

He forgot about the macho bit, hunkered down beside
her, shrugged amiably, and giggled. She glared at him.

"Don't know about the fingers and stuff," he said.
"About the fat, I think the idea is you get these cold savan-
nah nights . . ."

"Fur would be much better for that. Yes I know, we lost
our fur because we got too hot running after antelopes and
things. But in that case why didn't any of the others?
Cheetahs and so on? Losing fur's a rotten way to stay cool.
Look at the amount we've got to sweat compared to other
animals . . ."

"I don't know . . ."

"Well, you ought to, and what's more . . ."

He laughed again. It was difficult to be angry for long with him. They were still arguing when Michael called to him to empty the barrow.

"Finished?" muttered Dad.

"I'm sorry. It just came out. I'll think of something else next time."

"I thought you were going to try him on the shells."

"I'm sorry."

"Here's some more, anyway."

She took the pieces and sorted them through. There were two more from one of the larger creatures, and one of them fitted exactly onto a piece she already had. Now, from the curving growth-lines, she could see how the others might go. Sorting through the bag again, with eyes that knew what they were looking for, she found several chips she had missed first time, making up two complete patches and a few outlying bits. Laid out all in place on the ground they let her imagine the whole shell.

Feet crunched and a shadow moved on the sunlit slope.

"What are you up to, Vinny?" said Dr. Hamiska.

"I was putting this shell together so that Watson could tell me what it was."

"I can't have you distracting my work force, young lady."

Vinny looked across and saw that the barrow was almost full again.

"I was trying to stop him from distracting Dad," she muttered. "Can't you do something about it?"

Dr. Hamiska crouched to bring himself nearer, and whispered like a spy in a thriller.

"I'm afraid Sam's going to have to put up with him. Watson's uncle is Minister of the Interior. But I give you permission to distract him when he's not actually working. In fact I'll give you a hand."

He winked at her and took out his magnifying glass. Rather obviously playacting he picked up the largest piece of shell and pretended to study it as Watson came strolling across.

"Vinny's doing a fine job here," he said. "She was asking me how the shell came to get broken . . ."

"Rocks rolling around, maybe," said Watson. "You get a lot of that in earthquakes."

"But there aren't any rocks in the fossil layer," said Vinny. "Couldn't—"

She stopped, suddenly aware that something had changed. Dr. Hamiska wasn't playacting anymore. He passed the shell and glass up to Watson.

"Do you see what I see?" he said. "Sam! Can you spare us a moment?"

Wearily Dad climbed out, ducking under the awning, and came over. Watson whistled astonishment. Dad took the shell and looked at it for a while through his own glass.

"There could be a number of explanations," he said slowly.

"Oh, Sam! Sam! You're impossible! If the skies opened and the host of heaven appeared announcing the end of the world, you'd say there could be a number of explanations."

"Such as me having gone off my rocker. And I understood the end of the world was scheduled for Thursday."

"What is it?" said Vinny. "Please can I look? Don't tell me."

"Why not?" said Dr. Hamiska. "If an unschooled eye can see it, perhaps even Doubting Sam will begin to believe."

Vinny focused the magnifying glass on the outside of the fragment, near one edge, where she'd seen the others looking so intently. There were two sorts of markings on the shell, a series of waves or rumples running from the middle of what had been the hinge side across to the outer lip, and then a lot of finer bands running parallel to the lip, like tree rings, laid down as the shell had grown and grown. With the glass she now saw that these bands were interrupted by three small pits near the corner closest to the hinge, while on the very edge was a place like a chip on the edge of a china plate, when it's been knocked against something.

"Something hit it," she said. "It wasn't just squashed."

"Or someone," said Dr. Hamiska.

"You can't say that yet," said Dad.

"I say someone," said Watson. "Yeah, I'm with Joe. Look, just these three strike marks, all close, and the one on the break . . . Let's see."

He knelt to inspect the rest of the shell, looking slowly at each piece in turn and putting it back in its place before picking up the next. By the time he'd finished some of the others had arrived, and were passing the first shell fragment around. The air was full of tension.

"What about the piece the other side of the break?" said someone.

"I haven't found it yet," said Vinny.

"No more strike marks on any of these," said Watson. "Looks like it must've been, you know, deliberate, uh?"

Chatter broke out, excited, wondering. Vinny stared at the broken shell, working out what Watson had meant. Yes. If whatever had caused the marks had been accidental —stones rolling down in a landslip, say—then you'd have expected them to be scattered all over the shell. If just one stone had hit it, there'd be only one mark. But if someone had been deliberately trying to break it, they'd have hit it several times near the same spot, weakening it till it gave. Of course it could still be just coincidence, but . . .

"Quiet, everyone, quiet!" shouted Dr. Hamiska. "You know who we have to thank for this?"

Without warning he bent and picked Vinny up and set her on his shoulder like a three-year-old. The others cheered.

"That's twice now Vinny has brought us the sort of luck paleontologists dream of. Two miracles. One more, and the Pope will make her a saint. Till then the best we can do is call this site officially Vinny's site, and I shall see it goes into the reports as that."

Vinny managed to smile, but it was at this point that she definitely made up her mind she didn't like Dr. Hamiska. He'd been kind to her, and friendly, but that certainly didn't give him any right to treat her as if she belonged to him. And when he put her down he patted her on the head as if she'd been a spaniel or something. No.

Vinny cooked supper out of cans and Dad at least pretended to think it was delicious. They ate in the tent by the light of an oil lamp, with the netting down over each end, because without that all the insects in Africa would have been swarming around the light. As it was Vinny could hear the continuous faint flutter of tiny bodies batting against the net and the sides of the tent. It was wonderfully peaceful, and cool enough for a sweater. Dad was transferring the rough notes he'd made on the site into his main notebook, and Vinny was having another go at drawing her fossil, though her eyes were tired and the light was too poor for her to see the fine detail. Neither of them had spoken for half an hour. Dad closed his notebooks and looked up.

"Early bed for me," he said. "I'm worn out."

"Me too. And I can't see to draw."

"I think I'll have to tell Joe about those scratch marks you spotted."

"Oh. I suppose you've got to."

"What's troubling you?"

"Well, you see, I found it in the first place. I'm afraid he'll say it's the third miracle. I hate it when he makes a fuss about me like that."

"I thought you were relishing it."

"Well, I'm not. And I'm not his lucky mascot either."

"Um. I'll sit on it till you've gone. I can pretend to notice the marks then. I can certainly do without another bout of wild speculation."

"Thanks. I warn you, Dad, you'd better tell him as soon as I've gone. Otherwise I shall use it to blackmail you."

"Oh huh? What will be your price of silence?"

"I'm going to buy the sea-ape book and send it to you, and you're going to have to read it and tell me what you think."

His mood changed. He had been stretching and half yawning, relaxed, happy with her companionship, with being her father, but as she spoke she saw him shrink into himself and go cold.

"I'm sorry," she said. "I know I shouldn't have talked about it to Watson. It was stupid of me."

"It's done now."

"May Anna says . . ."

She stopped, knowing she'd put her foot in it again. She'd been going to tell him what May Anna had said about the sea-ape theory being wrong, but not crazy wrong. That would be a disaster now.

"Well?"

"May Anna says it's no use trying to pretend with you. I must just be what I am, and hope. So must you."

He looked at her and nodded.

"All right," he said. "Let's hope."

Then

For the first time, ever, in countless generations, the pattern of the tribe's existence changed. Accidents might have varied their journeys before—a storm, or a stranded fish large enough to feed them all for an extra day or so, keeping them longer in one place—but they had always tended to make the time up, reaching the river in the north around the new moon, and returning to the shrimping beaches at the full. Now they didn't go north at all. The first haul of fish lasted them three days, and then the dolphins came again.

This time the shoal was smaller, but the people knew what to do, so the catch was almost as great. Li hadn't called to the dolphins in her mind, but Presh assumed she had and took her out to dance with them when the hunt was over. Four days later the people were hungry again, but by then he felt that his leg was strong enough for normal swimming and he took them south.

To Li's surprise, though the rest of the tribe took it that she'd sent for them, the dolphins brought a shoal to a bay like the one where Greb had danced

after his fight with Presh. There was no bar to trap the fish
here, so the people lined up in the water in an open-ended
ring, into which the dolphins herded the fish to be
scooped out onto the shingle. Already these hunts were
becoming part of the tribe's life pattern, something which
happened because it happened, no cause for wonder at all.

Li did wonder. At times she was almost paralyzed by the
wonder of things—her own shadow, for instance, moving
below her as she swam above sunlit sands, or the intricacy
of a jellyfish, or why gulls could fly and she couldn't. She
wondered often about the dolphins, though she knew they
were so wonderful that she would never understand them,
unless, perhaps, when she died and they took her to the
place the sun came from.

(There were limits to her wonder. It didn't, for instance,
occur to her to wonder how both people and dolphins had
learned so quickly to help and trust each other—whether,
perhaps, in the thousands of generations during which the
people had roamed these shores this way of hunting had
been evolved, and then for some reason forgotten, but
with the memory of how it was done still lying buried
among the genes of both species until Li's chance meeting
with the first dolphin had revived it. Perhaps. But all Li
knew was that the dolphins felt like friends, and were wonderful.)

The tribe gave her time to wonder. They accepted that
she was part of Presh's glorious feast-providing leadership,
so they made a place for her in their life pattern. Presh
took her with him when he visited the families, and shared
with her the food they offered him, and that seemed right.
They remembered the birth ritual and insisted again on
her presence, demanding a plaited cord of the mother's
hair, to be threaded through the hole in whatever ornament the father brought. (A mother who owned a good

ornament, and whose baby was now old enough to be losing its birth fur, might find two or three males begging and bribing her to pass the thing on.) They showed Li their hurts, which mostly she couldn't do much for, though sometimes she stanched a bloodflow with a pad of seaweed which they could hold in place till the clot formed. And they gave her space when she chose to be alone, so that a mother might cuff a child who pestered her, as if she'd been a senior male.

But at other times, in squabbles over food, for instance, she might have a morsel snatched from her hand by a senior, as if she had no status at all. This seemed natural to her. She'd be angry, not affronted.

Presh wanted her nearby because he had to use every means he could to enhance his own prestige. His leg had mended crooked, turning his foot under him as he walked. He could swim well enough, but the muscles tired on long journeys and the foot didn't thrust well against the water. They all knew that he would never be able to perform the confrontation ritual for more than a few exhausting leaps, and that if it then came to a land fight he would certainly lose. So he had to make his own position so secure that no other male would want to confront him, unless he were half mad, like Greb.

He didn't consciously plan this. He was a sociable person, so it was natural to him to pay attention to the other senior males, to visit all the families and so on. Nothing he did was out of the ordinary. Only the result wasn't ordinary. The nature of leadership had changed. It now depended less upon dominance and more upon consent. The tribe had helped in the change by their refusal to accept Greb as Leader, and Presh's injury forced him to adapt to his limitations, and to control the tribe with the help of the seniors, male and female, and to see that stomachs were seldom empty. This was why Li was important to him. If times had been hard and food scarce, then the tribe would have let him go and accepted whoever had challenged and outfaced him. But with the living easy they were happy with things as they were.

Sometimes the dolphins stayed away from one full moon to the next, and the tribe would return to shore harvesting, but even then, because they'd had fish to eat last time they passed by, the mussel beds would hold succulent big mussels and the rocks and pools and crannies would be rich in crabs and octopi and other prey that had bred there undisturbed. Then perhaps three times in a journey the dolphins would herd shoals to them. Both sides were learning. A single dolphin would come swimming near the shark watch, filling the sea with its song, and answers would be heard, far off and faint. The shark watch would cry their new call, *Dolphin,* and the single dolphin would leave and Presh would collect everyone to the best hunting place on that stretch of shore, to wait for the driven shoal.

There was, for instance, a beach with a sand spit running out into the sea and the sea floor almost level beside it, drying right out at low water, but excellent when the tide was half full. The best swimmers would go out to help herd the shoal into the trap, others with Presh in command would wait on the sand spit, while everyone else lined up opposite it, standing close together in the water. The dolphins would herd the shoal in, the people on the spit would plunge in and close the trap, and then the line would carefully tighten, body against body, forcing the fish into a packed and threshing mass in the shallows where those no longer needed in the shorter line could wade, grabbing and flinging the helpless fish up onto the beach. Sometimes the line broke under the pressure. Sometimes the fish were small enough for many of them to slip through. But when the hunt went well they could catch all they and the dolphins needed in a single drive.

Days, times, seasons passed. The rains came for their usual few blissful days, heard first as thunder out to sea, then seen as banked clouds on the horizon and at the same time sensed in tension and waiting, the sky losing its blue and the air sticky, heavy to breathe, as if it were halfway to water. Finally the downpour smothering sea and land. A few days of that, leaving the sky sparkling, while the cliffs clothed themselves in green and the dunes behind the shrimping beach became a brief astonishment of flowers before the world settled back to heat and drought.

As the year went by Li felt the changes in her body begin which would make her ready to mate. Having watched slightly older friends go through the change, she was aware what was going to happen. It would be soon after the next rains, when all the land was clean, shining, new-made in the wetness, like a baby when first lifted from the mothering sea.

But those rains came early and different, without wait or tension or warning thunder. Instead the smoking mountain rumbled, and then was a night when the cliffs where they roosted seemed to quiver and rocks tumbled into the sea. At the caves the water had a strange taste. The dolphins didn't come.

Two nights after they'd left the caves, without warning, thunder crashed overhead. A huge wind lashed the coast. Lightning blazed from horizon to horizon with barely a blink of dark before the next dazzling shaft. Even that glare was veiled as the rain slammed down, loud as the pealing thunder. The world drowned. They breathed water as much as air. Dawn came, and they saw the sea churning against the cliff below in a broad, slow swell, ugly but swimmable. To them it seemed much more friendly than the racketing air. They made their way down and found that once below the surface they could forage easily enough, though the water itself felt strangely chill.

By mid-day, though they couldn't see the sun, the waves were beginning to rise, and the rain and thunder were no less. These cliffs were dangerous in such a sea, tricky to leave or land on, or to forage along. They would have to go elsewhere. South lay more cliffs, some of them safer in a storm, but only ledges to roost on as exposed as these. That was why, when Presh went around the families making signals to leave, they were ready to follow him back north to the water caves.

They came there without more trouble than could be expected from such seas, and though it was still light, crowded into the caves and huddled together shuddering from the unfamiliar rain-chilled air. That night the cave trembled and rocks fell from the roof and they woke and rushed in panic out into the open, but the rain was still pelting down, so when the trembling had been still for a while they went back in and slept until dawn.

They woke to the rising sun, a clear sky, and no wind, the only sounds the call of birds and the slow churn of waves against the bar. The water at the back of the caves was now too foul to drink, but rain-fed streams and water-falls were running down the cliffs outside. As the sun rose the air stayed cool and fresh. But despite the calm and beauty of the day there was a fretfulness in the tribe. They hadn't yet forgotten their fear—fear not of something they knew as a familiar danger, like sharks or wave lash on rocks, but of things that were strange, different, wrong. These rains, so soon, so short. This quaking earth. This stinking water in the caves. Wrong.

They looked to Presh for leadership and Presh looked to

Li for help and she had none to give. So they spread out and began to forage for food, as usual without much reward on this scant shore, but Presh stayed by the bay. More than once he climbed out and scrambled up the rocks to a vantage point from which he could gaze seaward, sniffing the wind and staring out for signs of some fresh danger. From there he could also see the central mountain, no longer gently smoking but sending up a black tumultuous cloud which rose high in the sky before it was blown away southward.

He had climbed there again, taking Li with him this time, still trying to make up his mind whether it was now safe to lead the tribe south, when suddenly he shouted and pointed north along the shoreline.

Li looked. The tribe had all stayed fairly close, waiting for Presh's signal. Well beyond them she saw a number of black flecks in the water. She knew them at once. Not dolphins, not birds, but the heads of people swimming toward her. Strangers.

Now:
Wednesday
Morning

Vinny woke before dawn, when it was just light enough for her to see Dad's shadowy movements as he tried to dress without disturbing her.

"I'll come and help," she said. "I can wheel the barrow if you don't fill it too full. I'd much rather work now, while it's not so hot."

"If you really want to."

While they were climbing the hill the stars went out as if someone had turned off a switch. Only a few minutes later the sun's rim clipped the horizon. Dad hacked soil out and Vinny wheeled the half-full barrow down the slope (no problem) and lugged it back empty (hard work). It was already getting hot before Dad decided they'd done enough. They went down the hill and breakfasted in the slant shadow of the big awning. For a while Dad said nothing so Vinny was silent too.

"I've been thinking about what May Anna told you," he said.

"So've I."

"What was your conclusion?"

"I'm not going to choose between Mom and

you. Not if I can help it. Mom tried to make me and I
fought her off. That was okay. But I can't fight you—it
wouldn't work. We've got to agree."

"Right. I'm going to make one condition though. You
are not to mention your sea-ape theory again to anyone in
this camp."

"Oh . . . all right."

"It's not because I think it's nonsense, though at the
moment I do. Someday, if you still want me to, and if I've
time, I'll read up enough about it to give you a considered
opinion, but not now. It's not in itself that important, but
the atmosphere on this expedition is already quite trying
enough for me without Joe or Fred or anyone having the
extra leverage of being able to needle me about it. I'm
afraid I'm not at all good at that sort of thing. I don't want
to have to cope with it now. Understand?"

"Yes, of course . . . only . . ."

He looked warningly at her.

"It's all right. I'm not going to talk to anyone about it. I
promise. If anyone asks me, I'll say I think it's nonsense
too."

"You don't have to go that far."

"It doesn't matter. Only . . . you know those toe
bones? I suppose Joe's taken them back to the camp."

"He won't let them out of his sight."

"If you find another one, will you look at it and try and
see if it might have been, you know, webbed? You needn't
say anything to anyone. Just look."

He thought about it and nodded.

"That's fair," he said. "Mind you, I think it's highly
unlikely, even if that were the case . . . and you'd probably need laboratory equipment . . . All right, I will try
to look as objectively as I can."

"Thanks."

"Not at all. Your mother in your position would have expected me to take on the lot of them in your cause."

"I'm not Mom."

"I am aware of that. But yesterday, for instance, when you were arguing with Watson about your theory and all I could hear was your voice, I had to keep reminding myself of the difference. And at times you look quite extraordinarily like her when I first knew her."

"I've seen the photographs at Gran's. Did you love her then?"

For a moment she thought she'd put her foot in it again, but he smiled without apparent effort.

"Since you arrived I've been reminding myself that we had two or three very good years before things went wrong."

"What did you call her?"

"Debbie."

"That's nice."

"She had something I felt I needed. More than just liveliness. A real excitement with life, a delight in its promises and possibilities, a readiness to plunge in, to take emotional risks. Conviction."

"What did you give her?"

"Not enough. I think she felt she needed a stable center, reliability, levelheadedness, a stone to strike her sparks off. I am a doubter, I see at least two sides of every question, I am emotionally cautious, organized, orderly. I felt myself becoming a silence for her to fill with words, an emptiness for her to pour her life into. I think. It's difficult to place things such as feelings, and changes of feelings, into their exact time. I've been tending to say to myself (and to other people, to be honest) that we should never have married. We were too different. There was no bridge between us. But that's not true. You've made me remember that there was a perfectly good bridge for a while. We let it fall down and then we couldn't find a way of rebuilding it, but it was there."

"Was it me made things change?"

"Of course you made things change. There were two people now in your mother's—Debbie's—life for a start, but you didn't bust the bridge, if that's what you mean. We did that. I think even before you were born, while she was still pregnant . . . I should never have let her call you that ridiculous name."

"I'm used to it. It's me now. Did you have a fight about it?"

"I'm bad at fights. I don't remember exactly. I expect I said 'Well, if that's what you want,' and left it to her."

"I can't imagine being called anything else now. Of course I hated it when some kids found out I was really Lavinia and started calling me 'Lav.' I'm no good at being needled either."

"Watch out for Fred, then. He's got a tongue like an asp."

"I guessed."

He grunted approvingly and they fell back into companionable silence, Vinny feeling that the damage she'd done yesterday had been repaired—more than repaired. Like a broken bone that's mended well, the link would be stronger than before. Dad had put his mug down when the immense and empty silence around them was broken by the gear change of the truck nosing down to cross the dry riverbed. He stretched and sighed.

"End of idyll," he said. "Let's let Joe find us at work. I think it's going to be hot."

"It can't be hotter than yesterday."

"I'm afraid it can."

★   ★   ★

Vinny and Dad had just reached the trench when the truck stopped below. Vinny watched the party climb out, the Hamiskas, Michael, Dr. Wessler, Nikki, and three or four others she'd scarcely met so far.

"He hasn't brought Watson," she said.

"That's something," said Dad. "Well, let's let him find us hard at it."

In fact he'd scarcely loosened his first trowelful from the fossil layer when Dr. Hamiska came striding up the hill, shouting good mornings, and peered in under the awning.

"Great work, Sam. You've shifted a lot. Found anything?"

"Hardly started on that. We were doing the heavy stuff before it got too hot. Vinny's been carting the soil away. We've been at it since sunrise. I see you haven't brought Watson."

"Your every wish catered to, Sam."

There was something in the tone of the remark, or perhaps the laugh that followed it, that made Dad look questioningly at him.

"It was his idea, Sam," said Dr. Hamiska. "We were talking about Vinny's shell last night and I said it would be useful to have an accurate identification. Dating, you know. Something to tell the Craig people. 'Some kind of Myaceae' sounds a bit feeble. Watson offered to drive back to his department and get the references."

"They won't have that sort of thing here."

"He's got access to the university computer. He can call up a databank. It would take me or anyone else a week to get permission."

"He'll tell everyone what we've found."

"No way I could stop him, Sam, seeing whose nephew he is. I don't want Wishart turned back at the airport. And it's not that much of a risk—if Watson's the only paleontologist in the country, who's going to listen or understand? And in any case, anyone who knows him will reckon he's shooting a line."

"Well, it's done now. Okay, Vinny, I'll be wanting the A-layer bag."

The morning wore quietly on. It was at least as hot as yesterday, and Vinny found it even more shattering. She'd been hoping to get used to it fairly quickly, but now she realized she'd be lucky if she did before she left. Dr. Wessler was in the second trench, beginning to work his way into the fossil layer the way Dad had done, and Vinny looked after both lots of bags and labels. Michael and another African called Ali started to clear the topsoil for a third trench, further along, while Dr. Hamiska and Nikki made a systematic series of shallow excavations all along the sloping line of tuff, trying to chart how far the fossil layer extended. Mrs. Hamiska drifted over the plain below, just looking.

Dr. Wessler was held up by a crocodile jaw jutting sideways into his trench. It was large but fragile, so that he had to scrape around it and burrow into the side wall, hardening it section by section with resin as he went. Dad found pig teeth, the leg bone of a small deer, and in the second section of H layer some fragments of another clam, and then more in the third section. There were no hammer marks on them, but when Vinny did a jigsaw with them she found that though there was still a lot missing the chips near the center were the smallest and seemed to make a sort of star pattern with a crack curving around it, just what you might get, she thought, if the shell had been broken first go, with one good bash. The actual point of impact was missing, but those chips would be tiny, so perhaps Dad had missed them. He was tipping the loose soil from the fossil layers separately on a plastic sheet, to be sieved through later.

"Can I have a look in your bucket, Dad, if you're not using it?"

"Hold it."

The words were little more than a murmur, but she could hear something in them, total absorption, interest, excitement. Ducking under the awning and peering into the trench, she saw Dad crouched below picking the clay away, crumb by crumb, from around a little cylinder of fossil.

"Is it a toe bone?"

"Looks like it."

"Don't forget about the webbing."

Grunt.

"Shall I get Joe?"

"Five minutes."

But Dr. Hamiska was already there. Usually he made a point of crunching around in his heavy boots as if he wanted to tell the world that the great Dr. Hamiska was coming, but this time he must almost have tiptoed down. He leapt off the boulder beside the trench and squatted by the awning.

"Got it sorted out now, Sam," he said. "What we've got must be something like a streambed running into the lake. There's just this nine-meter stretch. You're near the top of it—there's nothing beyond the boulder here—and it peters out just beyond the new trench. That's all. Just this one needle in the haystack, and we've found it! How are you doing?"

"Come and look."

Dad hardly had time to stand aside before Dr. Hamiska was in the trench, gazing at the new fossil, touching it with his forefinger, peering through his magnifying glass.

"Terrific!" he said. "I knew it was there! I knew it! This'll show 'em. Fred! Fred! Come over here! Someone tell Jane!"

He climbed out and waved his cap and hallooed to Mrs. Hamiska, who heard him, waved back, and started to come. By the time she arrived everyone else had had their turn to crouch and gaze and revere the tiny object, and now they were standing around, oblivious of the battering sun, talking like kids after a concert. In the middle of it all Dr. Hamiska laughed as if he'd thought of a new joke. They looked at him.

"And Sam didn't want to tell me!" he crowed.

"What do you mean?" said Dad.

"I heard Vinny ask if she should fetch me and you said no."

"Oh, rubbish," said Dad.

"I'm not deaf, Sam."

Dad gave an exasperated sigh but said nothing.

"It wasn't like that," muttered Vinny.

"Of course it wasn't," said Dr. Hamiska. "But I must insist that the moment any object of significance comes to light I am immediately informed, and that no further excavation takes place till I have seen it."

"Are you suggesting that I was in some way trying to keep this to myself?" said Dad.

"My dear Sam! Don't be so touchy. Everyone can keep in mind what I've said and we'll say no more about it. Now, let's imagine a stream running out of the hills, from roughly that direction. There has recently been a volcanic eruption which has altered the course of the stream into a new channel. It deposits its silt here for a number of years and then alters its course again, but in the meanwhile a number of creatures have died, leaving their bones to be preserved in the silt layers. One of them is our friend here.

She dies. Her body lies in the water. The flesh decays. The skeleton falls apart. The flow of the stream gently sifts the bones, scattering them in a regular pattern before the silt layers harden and hold them. We come along and find three points in that pattern. Can we from those three points deduce the rest of it?"

For a moment he made it sound actually possible. Dad shook his head unbelievingly. Dr. Wessler giggled.

"It's a lovely line, Joe," he said. "I hope John Wishart buys it."

Dr. Hamiska ignored him, entranced by his vision.

"Sam?" he said. "You're the taphonomist."

"Not a hope," said Dad. "For a start, it needn't have been a stream, and if it was how can we yet tell which direction it came from? I'd need to get the whole area cleared and mapped and do a series of computer simulations, and even then the best I'd be able to show you would be some probability curves. But if you want to tell Wishart that there was a stream and that the creature was female and died of hiccups on a Thursday afternoon, I'll keep my mouth shut."

Everyone laughed. The argument seemed over as soon as it had started, and the others went back to their work. Vinny looked at her shell fragments, but felt too worn out with heat even for something as simple as that, so she sat in the shade of the awning, looking out over the shimmering gray plain and trying to imagine it with water, and reeds, and pigs, and crocodiles, and something (someone?) sitting where she was sitting, looking out over it then. Dad seemed not to have noticed she was there, but he must have, because he spoke without looking around.

"It's all so unnecessary." He sighed.

"I suppose he wants to find everything himself. He's got to make it his, somehow."

"What have you done with that shoulder blade?"

"It's in the tent, with my drawing things."

"We'd better get it back into its bag. I don't want any more fuss. This evening, after he's gone."

"All right. I'm going to go and lie down, Dad. It's too hot for me. Listen, I've made another sort of shell shape. It's out here."

"Let's have a look."

He climbed out, studied the pattern with his head on one side, and grunted.

"Okay, I'll show Joe," he said.

"I thought there might be some of those little middle bits still in the bucket."

"Okay, we'll put it through a sieve. Well done. I suppose."

Wearily Vinny went down the hill.

Then

The tribe were still straggling out of the water in answer to Presh's bellows of *Come* when he limped along the beach to confront the strangers. There was a code for such a meeting. Although nothing like this had happened before in their memory, deep in their instincts, inherited through tens of thousands of generations, was a knowledge of what happened when ape group met ape group at the edges of adjoining territories.

The grown males went forward, their leader at the center. The females and young watched from behind, screaming defiance. The males displayed at each other, fangs bared, manes bushed, bellowing not their ritual challenge calls, but older ones, a hoarse repetitive bark which till now they had not known they knew. All this happened, much as it once had happened in the forest.

Li had come down with Presh from the rock from which they'd first seen the strangers and had joined the females as they'd gathered behind the line of males. Then, because it was difficult in the crush to see what was happening, she had gone aside and, much as she had done at the shark hunt, had climbed a little way up a gully behind the bay till she reached a point from which she could watch everything. The two groups of males were confronting each other, Presh with a whole line of them supporting him, but the other Leader with only three and those barely fully adult. The Leader, though, looked bigger and stronger than any male Li had ever seen.

What would have happened in the forest was that the smaller group, seeing they were outnumbered, would have been cowed and so retreated, and the larger would, if they'd wanted, have followed them until they began to feel they were getting uncomfortably far from their known territory, and stopped. A new frontier would have been established.

This was not how it went on the shingle beach. The three younger strangers indeed looked uncertain, and their manes began to flatten, but their Leader gave a louder bellow and took a pace toward Presh with his left arm raised into the fighting grip but his right swinging loose and low, as if he couldn't use it. The movement and pose made Li recognize him. He was Greb.

Instantly she was sure he had come for her. Terrified, she turned and scrambled further up the gully, which was still streaming with water after the downpour. The yells from below changed note. She stopped and looked over her shoulder.

Presh had limped forward to face Greb, also in the fighting pose, both hands raised. They were barely a pace apart. Greb moved a half step to the left and struck with his raised hand. Presh seized him by the wrist and struck with his other hand to grasp Greb's neck. Greb swayed away, but as he did so his dangling arm swung back and around. He had kept it till now with its back facing his opponent, concealing the rock he was holding. The blow caught Presh full force on the side of the skull. His head jerked violently away. He staggered half a pace back and toppled over. He didn't rise.

A moment's silence. Out of it Greb's bellow of triumph rose echoing around the bay. He stood punching the air, his right hand still grasping the rock. His three followers moved forward, their manes fully bushed out once more, and now Li saw that they too each held a rock. This was something that didn't happen. The whole ritual of challenge and contest was deep in the instincts of the males, preventing the kind of fighting to the death which might leave even the winner too badly hurt to survive, or at least to become a useful Leader. But Presh was dead.

The sheer shock overwhelmed the tribe. Even unarmed there were more than enough males to overcome Greb and his small group, but when Greb, still in his triumph posture, stepped forward to face Kerif, Kerif's mane at once went flat and he backed away. Greb paraded along the line facing them down in turn, daring them with threatening little movements of his rock to show the least sign of challenge. His followers copied him but stayed close behind him, not risking confrontation with the larger males of the tribe alone. Still further back the small group of females who had come with him watched apathetically. They looked cowed and miserable. They had no small young with them. Memories of ancient instinct told Li that Greb, somehow taking over the Leadership of such a group, would have seen to it that any babies they carried died. This was how it had happened in the forest long ago, though it didn't in the tribe.

As their males retreated in front of them the females of the tribe began to scatter in alarm. Some hurried for the water, others into the caves, others along the shore. Li saw

Ma-ma below, with the baby clasped protectively against her and Hooa beside her. She called, and again, and again. Ma-ma heard her, stared around bewildered, and at last looked up and saw her. Li beckoned, saw Ma-ma begin to climb, and immediately turned to scramble further up the gully. The nightmare certainty that Greb had deliberately come for her, to take her over and own and control and mate with her as soon as she was ready, filled her mind. She had no idea where she was going, or of what lay above the cliffs. No one had ever been up there before.

It wasn't at first a difficult climb, but so steep that soon she was gasping and despite her terror was forced to stop and rest. Ma-ma and Hooa weren't far below, with others behind. Pursuers? Greb? No, he was still on the beach. He had begun to organize a kind of triumph ceremony, with his own followers and as many of the tribe as he had managed to round up lined along the shallows and himself getting ready to parade in front of them. Presh's body lay where it had fallen.

Seeing Greb thus occupied Li was able to climb on more calmly until she reached a place where the gully ended in a cliff-face down which the rain-fed stream fell in a veil of spray. Beside the waterfall hung a mat of gourd vine. Li climbed the side of the gully with difficulty and found that the cliff-face extended either way, almost sheer, without handhold or foothold. By now Ma-ma and Hooa had reached the foot of the waterfall and were looking around, still bewildered with shock. Li joined them and saw Goor coming up the gully behind. She looked at the mat of vine.

Sometimes young members of the tribe would play swinging games at the bottom of vines, though their mothers discouraged them because it was impossible to be sure how strong the strands were, and there were many falls. Occasionally adults would use the vines as a means of reaching birds' nests, but always tested them carefully before they did so. It didn't happen often, as birds along that coast had mostly learned not to nest in such places. The vine by the waterfall looked skimpy. Li tested it and it stayed firm. Gingerly she climbed. There were occasional jerks when a strand gave under her weight, but the mat as a whole held and she reached the top, panting.

Ma-ma came next, with the baby clinging around her neck. As soon as she was clear of the bottom Hooa tried to follow, but Li barked *Stop* to her, and Goor echoed the call and pulled her back. Ma-ma was in any case a good deal heavier than Li. When she was almost up strands began to give and the mat swayed in toward the waterfall. Li grabbed at the tangle and managed to cling on till Ma-ma came over the lip and lay gasping.

There, Li called, and signaled to Hooa to climb in a different place, close against the fall. Hooa was frightened, so Goor shoved her aside and took her place. He was heavier still, but the vine held and he reached the top, soaked by the spray from the fall.

Hooa followed, but there were several people now at the top of the gully waiting their turn. The panic of their flight from the beach was still strong in them. Despite yells of *Stop* from above two of them had begun to climb before Hooa was halfway up. Others followed. With a series of crashes the whole mat gave. Hooa was swung sideways, right into the waterfall, clinging to the remains of a main stem, while the rest of the mat tumbled down on the people below.

When the mat gave Li had tried to grab it as before and had almost fallen with it. Now, craning over the edge, she could see Hooa hanging in the fall, unable to move. The stem she clung to snaked over the edge and inland to a shapeless corky mass which was in fact the base stock of the vine from which each year it sent out fresh strands to clothe the cliff. Li went and studied the stem and guessed it was strong enough, but found Hooa's weight too much to allow her to move it sideways along the cliff. *Come help,* she called. Goor came, and then Ma–ma, and together they simply hauled on the stem, dragging Hooa up through the streaming water, until she reached the top.

The others were still below, calling anxiously. Without the vine the gully was a dead end. There was no way out, except back down to the beach. Li tried lowering the stem which Hooa had used over the cliff in a fresh place, but its end dangled out of reach above the grasping hands below. It would need to be longer. She followed it inland to a point where it branched from another stem and started to bite her way through. The sap was bitter, shriveling lips and tongue, like the juice of the gourds themselves, but she persisted until she could break the stem free. She washed her mouth out in the stream and tried the stem over the edge.

It reached, but the people didn't know how to climb a single stem. Their ancestors in the forest would have done it easily, but in their long sea centuries their feet had evolved, become paddlers and standers and lost the ability to grasp. They had to cling with their hands to the stem, making no attempt to climb, while their friends above hauled them to the top. Rasping on the cliff edge the stem quickly lost strength and broke when the third trip had scarcely started. They needed a mat of vine, not a single stem. Li went and inspected the base stock.

She found that the vine began as a single stem, twice as thick as her arm. This branched into other stems, which branched in turn and so on, forming the mat. The first stem was far too thick to bite through, but the wood where she felt it seemed fairly soft. She picked up a stone and began to bash the main stem, then turned, called to Goor to help and gave him the stone. While he hammered steadily at the stem she and Ma-ma and Hooa hauled at the vine itself until it gave. They dragged it to the cliff edge and lowered it. The broken strands now reached to the people below.

Again, of course, they tried to climb several at once, but this time they felt the mat giving, not because it was breaking but because the four people at the top weren't strong enough to hold the weight. They leapt clear. Li and the others just managed to cling on and reposition the mat, and now those below realized they had to wait their turn, and though they jostled to be next in line climbed one at a time. The last of them, Rawi, pregnant with Presh's baby, was halfway up when a new figure appeared in the gully. It was Greb. He must have heard the commotion up on the cliff and climbed up to drive these escapers back down onto the beach and under his control.

In terror Li tried to haul the mat out of his reach, yelling *Help*. The others joined in and the mat came up with a rush, bringing Rawi with it. Timidly Li returned to the edge of the cliff and peered over.

Greb was standing below, staring up, with his face snarling and his mane bushed out. Rapidly he scrambled up the side of the gully, as Li had done, and saw that there was no way further. He went back, pushed through the waterfall, and found that it was the same on that side. By now all the escapers had lined the cliff and were staring down. He balanced himself, displayed ferociously at them, and yelled his challenge, so terrifying a figure that despite being for the moment safe from anything he could do to them several of them backed away out of his sight beyond the cliff edge.

Then somebody found a stone and threw it. It missed,

but others did the same, forcing him to retreat down
through the waterfall into the gully. Yells rose. They kept
up a hail of clods and stones, hitting him several times,
until he backed out of range.

Some kind of commotion was happening on the beach.
He looked, displayed once more, briefly, and then went
scrambling down to reestablish his dominance over his un-
willing followers.

Now: Wednesday Morning

The tent was like an oven, so Vinny dragged her cot into the shade of the big awning. It was still roasting there, and it seemed impossible that she could sleep, but almost at once she did.

Vinny's dreams were dreams of heat, of a shimmering marsh which somehow she had to lead the others across. There was one safe path. If you stepped off, the crocodiles would get you. She was the one who knew the way. She walked confidently between the reed beds and the others followed. (What others? They were vague in her mind, but she knew they were there, though she mustn't look around.) Something on the path. A flat white bone with a hole in it—a sign someone had left for her. She stared into the mists ahead for her helper. No. And when she looked down again, the bone was broken. And she'd forgotten the path. If she looked through the hole, she would see it again. Someone behind her was reaching to take it away and she would be lost and the crocodiles were coming nearer. They knew . . .

She woke rigid with terror, heard the crunch of

boots on shale, Dr. Hamiska's jovial laugh, and then they were standing around her, great black figures against the glare beyond the awning. There was a sense of tremendous good humor about them, of things going really well, but still half in her nightmare she had a certainty that it wasn't real, that any moment it was going to break down into shouts and rage. She wanted to be alone, but they were all around her, too big, too black against the glare, staring, laughing, plotting something . . .

She forced herself properly awake and sat up.

"Lunch ready, then?" cried Dr. Hamiska. "Roast goose and all the trimmings? Cherry pie? Champagne?"

"I've been asleep," said Vinny crossly as she stood up, looked for Dad, and moved to his side.

"Feeling better?" he muttered.

"Yes, thanks. Have you found anything else?"

"A pig mandible. More shells for you to sort. Jane's brought in a deer femur with what could be butchery marks on it."

"*Are* butchery marks," said Dr. Hamiska. "Have faith, Sam. And that second shell of yours, Vinny—that's excellent. With the first, it is clear that the blows were deliberate. You can show them to Wishart tomorrow."

"Oh . . . but . . ."

"No need to be shy. Sam will explain the technicalities. Listen, everyone—I might as well get this clear now. Our most important guest tomorrow is not a paleontologist; in fact before he became an administrator, John Wishart specialized in early Flemish art. My spies tell me that if it weren't for the terms of the Craig Foundation he'd have closed the paleontology department down years ago. Now he's going to be glad he didn't, because we've got a really big find for him, which will help him put Craig onto the map. What we've got to do is make him understand that.

We've got to show him that he can sell our find to all those people out there who never knew they could get excited about a few old bones. And it's no use looking at me like that, Sam."

"I'm hungry," said Dad.

"And so am I, but this is next year's bread I'm talking about. You want to go hungry next year? What I'm saying is that it's worth doing anything we can to show John Wishart how he can make this find into big news for Craig. People out there—the slobs in front of the goggle boxes—show them a few old bones and tell them they are two distal phalanges and a metacarpal from a plantigrade simian four and a half million years old, and they'll switch channels. But show them a group of shells that have been deliberately smashed with a primitive tool, and tell them it was a schoolgirl on a visit who put them together—let them see her doing just that—and that's news. That's something they can imagine their own daughter doing. That's the sort of line we've got to take with Wishart's visit. You may not like it, but we're working in a field where salesmanship has to go hand in hand with scholarship. So as soon as we've eaten I'm going to go through with each of you exactly what you'll be doing, and what you'll say, when I bring Wishart around. I'll photograph you with the shells later, Vinny, when the sun's at a good angle. Right, folks, let's eat."

In fact in that heat all anyone wanted to do was nibble, and drink. They sat around, passing the latest foot bone from hand to hand. Michael, who usually spoke very little, told a story, about another dig a few years back, when a really important visitor had brought a girlfriend who wasn't at all interested in fossils but was determined to photograph a lioness with her cubs. It had been in a different part of Africa, with more local people around (there were almost none here), and they'd got used to the idea that these foreigners would pay for news about places where you could find the right sort of old bones. Michael, who could speak the language, had been told to spread the word that now the foreigners wanted a suckling lioness, and one was found, and the girl got her photographs, and the important visitor was absolutely delighted, but for weeks afterward locals were coming in with reports of a lioness who'd just given birth—sometimes they'd walked two days to get to the camp—and weren't at all pleased to be told that the foreigners were only interested in old bones again.

He was a first-class storyteller. There were lots of sly jokes along the way. He made you see what everyone in the story was like—the pompous visitor, the slinky girl-friend—so it took Vinny a little while to notice that Nikki, sitting slightly aside as usual, with his pad on his knee and his pencil in his hand, was actually drawing her. Their eyes met as he glanced up, and he laughed and passed the pad across. The drawing wasn't in his careful, exact, fossil style—it was more like a cartoon. It showed a sort of ape child sitting cross-legged and bashing a huge clam shell with a stone she held in her fist. The body was halfway between ape and human, but the head was com-pletely human, only too small.

"Is that me?" said Vinny.

"Best I can do," said Nikki.

"Look, Dad. Portrait of your daughter."

"A perfect likeness."

"You should have given her webbed fingers, Nikki," said a soft voice behind Vinny's shoulder.

She turned. It was Dr. Wessler. He was smiling amiably, but she knew that behind his sunglasses his eyes must be glinting with malice.

"Or do you think they'd have got as far as fins?" he added. "Eh, Sam?"

Dad stiffened. Vinny cringed. So Watson must have told the others about their argument.

"Yes, indeed, Sam," said Dr. Hamiska. "What is this perverse nonsense you have been allowing your daughter to propagate? I can hardly think you are showing a proper parental responsibility, you know."

Several of the others laughed. If Dad could have done so too, it would have been all right—but he couldn't.

"It's nothing to do with Dad," said Vinny. "It's a book I found in the library at home, and as soon as I asked Dad about it he told me it was nonsense."

"Don't you believe it, Vinny," crowed Dr. Hamiska. "Sam's a secret believer. He's going to set the scientific world ablaze by finding a fossil hominid thigh bone with unmistakably froglike elements about it."

"And write a best seller," said Dr. Wessler. "Have you got a title yet, Sam? What about *Me and My Gills*?"

"Oh, for God's sake," said Dad. "Didn't you hear what Vinny said? She found the damn book in the library."

They were just like kids at school, just like the ones who'd found out Vinny's real name and cornered her in corridors and chanted it at her. You know it doesn't matter. You know it's stupid. You know if you could laugh about it they'd leave you alone, and the worst thing you can do is burst into tears, which was what Vinny had done, or lose your temper, which was what Dad did.

He didn't swear or shout. He simply went ultracold and looked directly at Dr. Hamiska and said, "The book may be nonsense, but it is no more nonsense than some of the theories I have heard propagated about our finds in the last three days."

For a moment it was as though he had actually hit Dr.

Hamiska—no, as if he'd spat at him. Then the big laugh
bellowed out, and everyone pretended to relax as though it
hadn't happened. Vinny stared at Nikki's cartoon, not enjoying it anymore. She'd been thinking how Colin would
have liked it—hung it in the downstairs bathroom probably, with his other favorite joke pictures—but now she
knew she wasn't even going to show it to him. She felt
miserable. She'd really let Dad down. It wasn't because
they all thought the sea-ape theory was stupid—the actual
cause didn't matter—what mattered was that she'd landed
him in a corner where he found himself behaving in a way
he was ashamed of. She guessed he was the kind of person
who lay awake at night remembering moments like this
and feeling sick about them. Now, she thought, he was
probably wishing she'd never come.

When the others were getting ready to move back up
the hill, Dad muttered, "You don't have to come. No sane
archeologist would be digging in midafternoon in this
heat."

"I'm all right. I want to come. I'm sorry about what
happened. It was my fault for gabbing away to Watson."

"You couldn't have known. What's done is done.
There'd have been something else, probably. How do you
feel about this business of being photographed?"

"I was going to ask you if I had to. But that was before . . ."

"Forget about that. What's the problem?"

"It's Mom, you see. I don't want to have to go on fighting her every time I get a chance to see you. I don't want
her to mind. I don't want her to think I've had a terrific
time. I wasn't going to lie, exactly, but I was going to say
things like it was a pity we couldn't go on safari and how
hot it was. You know? But if I start getting my picture in
the papers . . . I don't know. It might be all right. It's

just I have this sort of feeling . . . besides not letting Joe think I've got to do whatever he wants. It doesn't matter now. I expect it'll be all right."

"No. If you choose not to be photographed, then that's your right. Do you want me to tackle him?"

"Won't he just blow up?"

"Very likely. He'll assume I put you up to it. Or at least he'll pretend to."

"I'll do it. I'll tell him I've got a headache. Colin says you can't argue with a headache."

"Colin hasn't met Joe."

Then

There were nine of them at the top of the cliffs, all except Goor from the group of females and young who had stood behind and watched the confrontation of the males on the beach. They waited for a while gazing down, trying to see what was happening below, longing to return to the safe, known shore, hoping perhaps that the males of the tribe would somehow realize their combined strength and unite to drive Greb away, as they'd done before. Li was still almost unable to think or move without terror, after Greb's sudden appearance at the head of the gully. She was convinced he'd climbed the cliffs deliberately to search for her. She didn't dare even show herself above the cliff edge, but hung back, gazing around, looking for a way of escape in case he came again.

Above the cliff the ground, stony and bare, sloped gently up to a crest, beyond which she could now see the central mountain pouring out its billowing black tumult of smoke. The rain-fed stream runneled down a shallow dip from the top. She knelt and drank and splashed some water over herself and then climbed beside it. Her main thought was still that if Greb came back she must have somewhere to hide.

The crest was not a true crest. The hill went on up, but then leveled and dipped into a cupped valley. At her feet spread a wide, still pool, collected from the surrounding hills after the torrents of rain, and still being fed from the further slopes and so still sending its overflow out and down over the cliff. Without hesitation she waded in and sank below the surface, and as she did so her terror left her. Greb could not climb the cliff. He was busy on the shore. He hadn't really come for her . . . The strange, un-buoyant water was like that of the freshwater pool, the place where the tribe had always felt most itself, most sure, most peaceful. She lay, looking up through the still surface at the blue and brilliant sky, until she had to rise for breath. She sank again and rested, rising and sinking, until the sense of loneliness and separation reminded her of the oth-ers and she went to look for them.

They were by the stream, splashing themselves and each other with water. Tilted toward the east, face on to the morning sun, the slope above the cliffs was already becom-ing hot as noon. Before long its surface would be painful to the touch. There was no shade. Their whole instinct was to try and find a way down to the beach, but their fear of Greb prevented them, and when Li appeared further up the stream, beckoning and calling *Come,* they followed her back to the pool and waded gladly in.

They spent the middle of the day there, but there was no food of any kind in this transient water, so as the sun slanted west they went back down to the cliff to try and spy out what was happening below.

People were moving around on familiar-looking activi-ties, foraging, and greeting. The sea was almost still, the air windless. Rawi cried *Look,* and pointed not down but along the cliff to where a solitary figure stood, also looking down. A male. Li's panic surged, then she realized that it wasn't Greb. Now he had seen them and came hurrying toward them. He turned out to be Kerif's younger half brother, Kadif. His head and face were all bloody and his left eye too swollen to open. He must have managed to climb the cliff further along.

As he came he pointed to the shore, and gave the *Danger* call, but there was no need. Already, twice, the watchers had heard floating up through the afternoon stillness, Greb's bellow of command, mad but triumphant. They climbed back to the pool and when night came huddled beside it, nursing their hungers.

In the dark the ground shuddered violently and they woke and heard the whole world groan and saw what they couldn't see by day, that the central mountain was shooting columns of gold and orange up through the massive smoke cloud, and throwing out immense golden fragments which arched aside and fell flaming onto the slopes below. The night air became colder than the water of the pool, so they moved into the shallows and waited there for the dawn.

When it came the mountain was quiet again, merely billowing smoke. Very hungry by now they went back down to the cliff. The sun rose, blazing across a waveless sea. They listened for the song that should have greeted it but instead heard only a single voice, Greb's.

It was clear to Li now that they had to get down to the shore. If Greb was still at the water caves, they must go elsewhere, before the sun became too hot, so that they could travel beyond his reach. She took Ma-ma by the hand, grunted *Come,* and started off, with the others trailing behind. The ground rose steeply toward a ridge which formed the southern headland of the bay. It would have been quicker to cut straight across, but their whole instinct was to follow as closely as possible the tribe's normal route along the shoreline below, so they continued on around.

On these higher cliffs nested colonies of sea birds, whose clatter and screams rose louder as the travelers neared, reminding them of their hunger, and of the taste of eggs and juicy nestlings. They stopped and peered over and saw the parents wheel away from the crammed ledges below. There was food there. Their mouths watered. Desperately they searched for a way down, but there was none.

Then, looking along the cliff, Li saw a gourd vine and remembered how they had used one yesterday to climb the final stretch in their escape. This one was bigger, its main stem half as thick as her own body, but she gave Goor a stone and showed him where to bash and set Kadif to do the same from the other side while the rest of them heaved together at the mat. In the end the stem gave, and they dragged the whole mat along and lowered it down to reach the nests, then climbed down one at a time to feed while the rest of them anchored it at the top or moved it along when a stretch of ledge had been cleared.

Li had just climbed back from her second feed when she heard a grunt of *Look,* and turned. Hooa was pointing out to sea, with egg yolk dribbling down her chin. The others peered and muttered surprise and puzzlement. There was a strangeness on the horizon. The sea from this height seemed a dead flat calm, as if it had been stretched taut all around its edges, but not as far as the eye could see. Far out, almost at the limits of vision, it changed, but they couldn't yet make out how.

Now all were staring. No one climbed down the mat. They muttered. Soon they could see that the whole line of the horizon had become like a low cliff, a far headland seen from another headland. It was strange. For a while it stayed like that, and they half lost interest and went on with their nest raiding until they realized that the strangeness wasn't just something that had risen from the sea, a long way out, but was coming nearer.

Now they knew what it was. There was a call used in the tribe at seasons when rollers came steadily in from the ocean but foraging was still safe, provided the foragers were aware of their rhythm and could judge the come-and-go of surges. The danger was that occasionally a pair of rollers would somehow double up and produce between them a monster, so at those times watchers were set at vantage points along the shore to call a warning when they saw a wave like that coming. *Big wave,* they muttered to each other. Yes. Big wave. Only, at first, seeing it from this distance and this unfamiliar height, they couldn't realize how big.

A hundred miles out across what is now the Indian Ocean, below the deep sea floor, the plates that carry the continents had moved. For ages they had been still, jammed, and so the tensions between them had grown and grown, and now at last something had given. In the continents on either side of the rift there had been earthquakes and eruptions, signaling the change. Then, as the plates had juddered to their new positions a whole section of the ocean floor had buckled into a line of underwater hills, and as it had done so it had set up an earthquake wave in the sea itself, the wave that is like no other wave and is called a tsunami.

It neared and neared, until even the watchers on the headland began to grasp something of its size and speed, and to realize the danger the rest of the tribe were in. They could see the others still, small dots in the distant bay, moving around. They began to call at the tops of their voices: *Big wave! Big wave!* Perhaps the tribe had already heard, like underwater thunder, the sound of its approach. They were coming ashore, lining the beach, safe from the largest waves of any normal sea.

Now those on the headland could make out the shape of the wave, a black steep hill, ridged and hummocked, though the ridges and hummocks were themselves enormous waves. White foam glittered along the moving crest. And now as its roots touched land it changed and rose and the hill became an inward-curving wall, black, hard, with a white mane of foam along the hanging ridge, poised to fall but not falling because the rush of the wave itself caught it up before it could do so. In front of it, along its length, was a trench or gulf where it sucked the calm ahead back into it, and now this too broke into roaring foam as its own roots touched land.

They cried aloud and pointed. Tiny with distance, ahead of the wave in the still, silky calm, dark specks appeared, and vanished and came again a few heartbeats later. A pattern of dolphins was racing to escape the wave, but for all their speed they were too slow. The watchers wailed in terror as they saw the wave engulf them. But now they knew its speed, and from that its distance and from that its size, and realized that even up here on the headland they might not be safe. They ran for the ridge behind, reached it panting, and turned.

By now the people in the bay had seen the wave, understood their danger, and were trying to escape. Some were perched on rocks, others climbing the gully which Li had used yesterday, but it was clear to the watchers that they would be too late. The wave was almost ashore. But time had slowed and it seemed for those last few pounding heartbeats to be loitering on its way, to be climbing as it came, to be reaching up and up, and forward too, as if it were deliberately leaning to claw the watchers from their hilltop. It reached the headland opposite and they saw it tower into the sunlight in an immense and glittering white column, growing and growing as the power that had driven it landward was forced to spend its unimaginable energy in upward motion, climbing until it seemed to be reaching for the sun.

Then it struck the headland on which they stood. Huge though it was its crest had come below these higher cliffs, so first they heard its thunder and at the same moment the blast of air expelled from between the wave front and the cliff hammered them to the ground. They wailed, and with the instincts of sea creatures who had learnt to survive on storm-battered coasts they limpeted themselves to the boulders which strewed the headland. Some closed their eyes, but Li was impelled to watch. Terrified, numb, certain of death, her need to know and wonder still had power.

She saw the white wall shot skyward at the headland, saw the wave pass by, rising as its mass was funneled into the bay, surging above the cliffs where they had passed, so that it would fling itself far up the slope beyond, where the stream had run, right over the pool and on up the mountainside, but before it did so the world around her went dark as the water of the wave's first onslaught began to crash back down.

Land creatures would never have survived it. It fell not as foam, not as ordinary wave strike reaching a shore, but as solid, immense slabs of the black, cold inmost ocean, slamming down. There would be a moment to breathe, and then another mass of water hammered against them, swirled around them, dragged at them where they clung, and roared away. Li felt the big rock to which she had anchored herself stir in its ancient bed and readied herself

to loosen her hold if it rolled away, but it settled back and
she was able to fasten herself to it again.

The first was worst. The higher the water had been
flung the more it broke apart in the air and fell back no
longer in solid slabs but first as a foaming torrent then as a
downpour, half air, half water, then as rain, and at last, for a
long while, as a fine salty drizzle, icy cold.

Bruised and gasping Li let go of her hold and sat up.
Ma-ma was already sitting, huddled over the whimpering
baby which somehow she'd managed to shelter beneath
her through the onslaught. Around them the others rose,
those that were left, for two had vanished, either battered
from their hold or because the boulders to which they had
clung had themselves been rolled down over the cliff. This
must almost have happened to Goor. He came limping up
the slope, shaking his head, having been knocked loose
and then by a miracle found somewhere else to cling before he was washed away. Below them the sea was a cloudy
turmoil heaving to and fro in an immense and shapeless
swell whose hummocks were only the ripples set up by the
shock of the tsunami striking the continent, but were
themselves large enough to send columns of spray squirt-
ing against the cliffs far higher than any wave Li had ever
seen.

Look, called someone, pointing. They saw, and gasped.
Behind the bay the last of the tsunami was still sheeting
back from the mountains beyond, but the ground over
which it fell in foam had changed. There were no cliffs
there anymore. The weight of the wave had smashed them
down into a tumbled slope of boulders, right across the
shore, right across the bay and out beyond the bar that had
sheltered it. Unreachable beneath that mass of stone the
tribe, and Greb, and the strangers he had brought, and the
water caves too, lay buried.

Now:
Wednesday
Afternoon

Vinny was scared of what Dr. Hamiska would say, and wanted to get it over, talking to him alone, so she had to wait till they all climbed the hill again. Still she didn't get a chance, as he kept loping around, seeing what everyone was doing—like a herd bull on a wildlife program, she thought, patrolling his territory to stop any interloping male from darting in and making love to one of his wives. His laugh, even, was like a bellow of challenge. If she hadn't been so nervous she might have had a giggling fit.

Then he went back up to the little cliffs and started to measure and take notes. He looked around and smiled as she approached.

"Just in time," he said. "Hold this end for me, will you? How are you bearing up?"

"I've got a headache. Is it all right if you don't photograph me with the shells?"

"Tomorrow will do. No, Wishart will be here tomorrow. It'll have to be Friday. Perhaps we'll have . . ."

He had been measuring while he spoke, but now he turned his head and stared at her. His voice changed.

"Or will you have a headache on Friday too?" he said.

"It's terribly hot. I'm not . . ."

"Sam put you up to this."

"No. What . . . ?"

She'd known he'd be angry, but still wasn't ready for what happened. Not that he shouted, or even said anything for a bit. He just pushed his sunglasses up onto his forehead and stared at her with his stony pale eyes, and it was like being hit by an invisible force, or like walking out of the shade of the awning into the African sun. He leaned slightly forward. She could see the whole round of each iris. He wanted her to flinch, to burst into tears perhaps, but it didn't work out like that, though it easily might have. It was Mom, in a way, who came to her rescue. Vinny had never before felt so like her, so surely her daughter. Mom wasn't afraid of anyone. She'd once got hold of the private number of the chairman of some firm which made power stations and radar towers, as well as her washing machine, and had rung him up in the middle of a dinner party and made him listen while she told him exactly what she thought of his organization for making her wait in all day for a service engineer who didn't come. Vinny felt just like that now. She was furious. Dr. Hamiska had no right to do this to her.

"I'm sorry," she said, "but I don't want my picture in the papers."

"Why on earth not? Unless Sam . . ."

"It's nothing to do with Dad. It's because of my mother."

"Are you serious, Vinny? I explained in words a child should understand how vital it is that this find should have all the publicity we can manage. What on earth can your mother object to? Is it some kind of religious hang-up?"

"No, of course not. But it's private. I'm sorry."

"You're sorry. Let me tell you, Vinny, that I have put myself out very considerably to accommodate your visit. It was ridiculous of Sam in the first place to suggest taking time off in the middle of a working season. As it was I had to arrange everyone's schedules to allow you as much time with him as possible. And now when I make a straightforward and harmless request for your cooperation over something of real importance, you tell me first that you've got a headache and then that your mother wouldn't like it."

He stared at her again and this time she found she had to look away.

"You seemed to have no objection earlier," he said. "When I was talking about the arrangements for tomorrow. Well, here's your father. Let's see if he can see you make sense."

Vinny turned. Dad was trudging up the slope. Beyond him some of the others had stopped work and were watching. They were too far off to hear anything, but they could see. When Dr. Hamiska erupted he let everyone know.

"Perhaps you can tell me what this is about, Sam," he said. "Vinny has come to me with some story about her mother not wanting her photographed."

"You've got hold of the wrong end of the stick," said Dad.

"You'd better explain."

Dad blew out an unhappy breath and shook his head.

"I'm afraid it's a private matter between Vinny and her mother," he said.

"I find that hard to accept."

"Do you imagine Vinny would say she didn't want to be

photographed, knowing you would like her to be, if she didn't have a very good reason?"

"If she has a reason, she can tell me and I will treat it with full confidentiality. Do you suppose I have nothing better to do with my time than broadcast schoolgirl secrets to the world?"

"Oh, for heaven's sake . . . !"

"I am trying to be reasonable, Sam. It seems to me that it is you and your daughter who are being unreasonable—in fact, deliberately obstructive, as you have tended to be all along."

"What on earth are you talking about?"

"I am talking about the fact that, for reasons I can only guess at, you have done your best, both overtly and surreptitiously, to undermine and thwart the objects of this expedition."

"I still can't imagine what you're talking about."

"Then I will give you instances. From the first you attempted to persuade your colleagues that we were on a wild-goose chase. You appeared to take your duties so casually that you suggested leaving us for two weeks to take your daughter on safari. You surveyed this site and reported it of no special interest, and when I recently proposed taking another look at it, you did your best to dissuade me. Then, as soon as I made a find of crucial importance, you suggested setting up a fly camp here so that you could work at it unsupervised. You then proceeded to carry out your excavations, on so-called professional grounds, with such painstaking slowness that—"

"That's unfair!" shouted Vinny. The cry had burst out of her. Dad glanced at her and shook his head. Dr. Hamiska ignored her.

"With my own ears," he said, "I heard you attempting to conceal from me that you had uncovered another hominid fossil. Even now, with your daughter's help, you are attempting to see that our find is denied the publicity it needs for me to raise the funds to conduct a full-scale excavation of this site next year. Do you need me to point out what the pattern of your behavior seems to add up to?"

Dad shrugged and half turned away.

"What conceivable motive . . . ?" he began, and stopped.

"I'm afraid your motive is perfectly obvious, Sam. I deeply regret it. But in the meanwhile you are suspended from all further work on this site. I want you to collect your own personal equipment and then not set foot inside the marker posts. The same must apply to your daughter. You can pack up the fly camp and return the jeep to the main camp. We will discuss your position after Wishart's visit."

"It needn't wait till then," said Dad. "I'm resigning now."

Dr. Hamiska nodded indifferently and turned back to measuring the rock strata. Vinny grabbed Dad's arm as she felt herself swaying. He steadied her against his side.

"I'll be all right in a mo," she whispered. "Sorry. Okay."

He kept his hand under her arm and helped her down the slope. She still felt sick, but the world felt steady and solid again. Everyone was watching. Dr. Wessler was waiting by Dad's trench.

"Had a bit of a bust-up, then?" he said, smiling thin-lipped.

"I'm off," said Dad. "Just come and check what I pack, will you? Tell him I'll have my notes in order for someone to take over by tomorrow mid-day. Nikki, just watch

Vinny pack up, will you? Look through her things. I want witnesses we're not taking anything off the site. Thanks."

Vinny had very little to pack. As she straightened and hitched her satchel onto her shoulder she saw Dr. Hamiska still at the cliff-face, measuring and taking notes, deliberately ignoring the scene below.

"Got what he wants," whispered Nikki. "Look how he's standing."

"But he really needs Dad. Everyone says so."

"Not anymore, maybe."

"Ready?" called Dad. "How are you feeling? Let's have your bag."

"I'm all right now."

They started down the hill.

"Oh, Dad, I'm sorry," said Vinny as soon as they were out of earshot of the others. "It was my fault. I shouldn't have made a fuss."

"No it wasn't. Though I don't think he was planning for it to happen just yet, not until after tomorrow, but he saw his chance and took it."

"I don't understand. And Nikki said he'd got what he wanted."

"That's about it. I hadn't realized. I imagined he kept winding me up because he couldn't help it."

"I still don't understand. May Anna said you really needed each other. She said he found the fossils and you worked out what they meant and people believed you."

"That's a way of putting it. Even now Joe knows I'm not going to try and persuade anyone that he hasn't found what he has found. I will confirm that if the geological data work out, he's made what may be the most important early hominid find since Johansson discovered Lucy in 1974. With that he can be confident of raising funds for a full-scale expedition next year. He can pick his helpers,

and that means that when it's over he can have his name at
the head of the papers describing the finds, without anyone else on the same footing. If he'd kept me on the team,
he'd pretty well have been forced to print my name alongside his."

"But that's mean. That's really mean!"

"I'm afraid it's the sort of thing that matters among
many scientists. It doesn't worry me. What does is that
now he is going to start putting it around that I had spotted
the importance of the site at an early stage and was trying
to keep it quiet in the hope that he'd fail to raise the funds
for another expedition, and I'd then be able to bring one
out myself."

"He can't. Won't anyone say . . . ? Dr. Wessler . . . ?"

"Oh, Fred will stir the pot. He likes trouble. Right. You
pack your stuff. We'll leave the tent and bedding and so
on . . ."

It didn't take long. Vinny was sorting out her drawing
kit when she found the shoulder blade.

"What shall I do about this, Dad? The H bag is still up at
the site."

"Oh, Lord. I don't know. I'm going to have to do a new
note on it. Bring it along and we'll give it to May Anna.
She can get it . . . No, I'll just leave it with the notes.
That'll do."

Dad said nothing on the journey. Vinny could almost feel
him thinking, the same exasperated ideas churning around
and around in his head as he drove. She dozed a few sec-
onds at a time, was woken by a jolt, and dozed again. Then
she must have slept longer because when she woke the
angle of the sun had changed and they were driving along

with hills on the left. They must be nearly there. She gazed around and saw a pale blue fleck far up the hillside.

"There's May Anna," she said.

Dad slowed to look and braked. Vinny leaned out and waved. May Anna waved back and began to pick her way down. Dad gave a sigh of exasperation.

"Can't we go and meet her?" said Vinny.

"I want to get back. I've got a load of work to do, and I'd like to finish it and go while Joe is still busy with Wishart. We've got a major discovery, and I'm not having Joe tell people I messed it up by going off in a huff, leaving everything in a mess. On the other hand, as soon as he's finished with Wishart he'll be wanting to pick it all over, just keep us hanging around to show he can."

Vinny could hear that these were excuses. Half excuses, anyway. They might be true, but just now he didn't want to talk to anyone, even May Anna.

"You go on," she said. "I'll wait for her. Can I tell her what's happened? She'll want to know."

"Yes, of course. Thanks."

He sounded relieved. As Vinny watched him go she realized it wasn't a case of not even May Anna. It was especially not May Anna. He'd actually faced up to Dr. Hamiska for Vinny's sake, but then he couldn't face telling his girlfriend about it. People are impossible to understand, she thought. They're just what they are.

It was late afternoon and still hot, but so much cooler than it had been out in the badlands that she decided to go and meet May Anna. It looked like an ordinary climb, with plenty of open spaces between the scrub, but the sun was in her eyes so that she couldn't pick her path more than a few paces ahead. She found some kind of an animal track going in the right direction, but it ended in a wall of thorny bushes, and when she turned to pick her way around she saw, only a few paces in front of her, coiled on a shelf of warm rock, a large brown snake.

She froze. It must have heard her about the same moment she'd seen it, and raised its head and hissed. They stared at each other. Vinny's heart thumped for action, but she seemed unable to move until the snake lowered its head and slid away quietly into the scrub.

"Where are you?" called May Anna.

"Here, I can't get any further."

"Go back down to the road. Meet you there."

Vinny pulled herself together. It was silly. The snake had been the only bit of wildlife she'd seen close up, and she ought to have been thrilled, not terrified. May Anna reached the road a few minutes after her.

"Hi," she said. "What are you doing, back now? Thought you were stopping out there."

"Dad's resigned."

"Oh, my! How'd that happen?"

Vinny started to explain. She thought she was in control but before she finished she began to cry. The stupid, childish sobs shook her, and she could feel her tears trickling through the layers of dust on her cheeks. May Anna crouched and put an arm around her shoulders.

"Joe can be a real bastard," she said. "I guess Sam's right —that's what he's been trying to make happen. It wasn't your fault, Vinny."

"But I started it."

"And your dad backed you up."

"He didn't have to. It wasn't really important."

"I bet it was too."

The sobs came under control. Vinny blew her nose and let May Anna clean her face for her. They walked back slowly toward the camp, with Vinny talking about what

had happened in bits and pieces, as they came to her. May
Anna clucked and muttered sympathy.

"And Sam left you to tell me," she said sadly.

"He wants to get his notes written up so we can leave
tomorrow."

"I guess so."

At the camp May Anna went and kissed Dad and patted
his shoulder. Vinny had stayed out of earshot, so she didn't
hear what they said, but it was only a few words. Then
May Anna fetched drinks for all three, and she and Vinny
went and watched the shadows stretch as the sun went
down behind them. They didn't talk much. May Anna was
obviously shocked and depressed by the news, and didn't
pretend about it.

"Can't you come with us?" said Vinny. "You'd cheer
Dad up. Me too."

"And me, but I can't, Vinny. I have to earn my own
bread. Joe's not a forgiver-and-forgetter. Either you're for
him or you're agin him. And this is really exciting stuff
here—if I'm in on it, that's my career made. I want to
come back next year. I'm sorry."

In the last light they heard the engine of the truck, then
saw its dust cloud, gray in the shadow of the hills and
golden as it rose into the sunlight. As it neared its horn
began to sound a triumphant, sneering da–didi–da–da.

"Bastard," muttered May Anna. "And he'll be jolly Joe
Hamiska too, all evening, I bet."

She was right.

Then

They crouched together, too shocked to stir, moaning over their hurts, gazing at the terrifying change, and then turning their heads away. Or they peered out to sea, in case another monster wave might be preparing. For a long while the upshot spray fell over them, like the finest of fine mist, but at last it thinned and blew away and the sun began to beat down full strength on the headland, forcing them to move. They crossed the crest and looked south to see the same weird ocean churning down the shore, familiar only in its broadest outline of headland beyond headland, but with all its detailed landmarks—outlying pillars, known cliffs, rock islets—changed and gone. In the end they made their way back down to the place where the bay had been, because they could see that at least they ought to be able to climb down there to nearer sea level.

The cataract which had been the backwash of the tsunami had diminished now into separate streams and falls, foaming down the tumbled rocks. In a crevice high up Rawi found a huge fish, as large as her own body, stranded there by the wave. They heaved it out and dragged it to a place where a fall tumbled onto a boulder and sent a continuous pleasant spray across a flat shelf beside it, and stayed there through the middle of the day, eating when they wanted, touching and stroking each other often, watching the dreadful swell slowly subside and restore itself to a steady pattern of waves, and gradually as they did so becoming used to the idea that they at least had survived, that the tribe was not gone, because they themselves were now the tribe, and that tomorrow would come.

Toward evening they started to explore, visited the sea and found it weirdly cold with the in-mixing of waters heaved from the sunless deeps, scrambled about the rockfall, discovered enough stranded fish to feed the whole tribe many times over, and came to a place where a section of cliff had fallen away whole and become propped across two other pieces, making a kind of cave where they could sleep. There they spent a restless night, waking each other by the cries of nightmare, clutching together for comfort and then moaning themselves back to sleep.

Li woke a little before dawn. She too had been redreaming the tsunami, but this time not with terror. The terror had come before, had been Greb. She had been alone on a shore and he had been advancing on her, his mane immense, like a black sun with his snarling face in the middle of it, and in her nightmare she'd cried to the dolphins, and the sea had simply risen around her at their bidding and swept Greb away, leaving her alone and safe on the beach. She had been waiting for the dolphins to return and dance with her, and woke with a pang of grief that they hadn't come. Yes, she thought as she woke, that was what had happened. It was the dolphins who had sent the wave. They had done it to save her from Greb. Hadn't she seen them racing in front of it, not, as she'd first thought, trying to escape it, but leading it on, showing it the way, having arranged for her to be safe on the headland? She didn't know why so many of the others had had to die too, but she accepted it because the dolphins had thought it was necessary, and they were wiser than she was. Still, it made her feel strange.

Kadif was now the natural Leader of the group, but he was hurt and unsure of himself. Goor was in no mood to challenge him. The others simply waited for Li to decide. She took them south. There were so few of them now that they could probably find enough food wherever they chose to forage, but with the water caves gone they must have somewhere else to drink, either the pool or the river to the north. The pool was a place of happiness, but at the river, without land watch or sea watch, they would be in great danger. There was no choice.

They went slowly, clinging to the unfamiliar shore, in almost constant alarm, each night having to find a new place to roost. On the third morning they came on the stranded dolphin. It lay far up one of the shingle beaches where the tsunami had tossed it, dead. Already the orange crabs had been out to scavenge at its body. Enormous numbers of them must have been killed by the tsunami, but some had survived. When Li first saw the body her heart leapt, because it seemed clean and undamaged, and she thought that if they could haul it back to the sea it would come alive and swim away, but moving closer she saw that the eye was a hollow pit, ravaged at the edges, because crabs had made their way in there and burrowed in the flesh beneath. When she touched the flank, which she had known as living flesh caressing against her in the song-filled water, she could feel the skin lying against the ribs with nothing at all beneath them. Shocked, appalled, she led the way on.

That night the true rains began. The earlier downpour had been a freak, perhaps connected somehow with the upheavals beneath the ocean. These, though they came without the days of tension before, were otherwise normal, heavy and steady, driven by the threshing onshore wind, lasting a few days and then passing away to leave a calm, clear sea and sparkling air. On the headland beyond the bay where the dolphin lay the group had found an excellent roosting place, where a fallen slab leaned against the cliff well above wave reach, giving them shelter from both wind and rain. With all they needed for drink falling direct from the sky, they stayed there and waited the rains out.

Before they moved on Li felt compelled to go back and look at the dead dolphin again. By now the crabs had stripped it completely and only the skeleton was left, a fine white structure, the arched ribs joined to the supple spine which ended in the snouted skull with its huge eye socket. To Li, dead though it was, and gone, it still seemed to have power. The empty eye looked as if it knew things she could never know. She saw, amazed, that it had a hand like hers. The long, thin fingers which had been hidden in the flipper now lay across the ribs, still joined to the stubby arm and shoulder blade. Some of the finger bones had fallen away. The shoulder blade was loose and when she picked it up the arm became separated from the hand, and then the arm fell away too, leaving her holding just a flat triangular bone. That would have to do. She would have liked to take the head, but it would be far too heavy and difficult. This flat bone would be enough. She carried it back to the others and led them on.

Beyond the next headland a fresh change began. If

they'd been traveling further inland they would have been
aware of it far sooner, a smothering layer of heavy gray
dust spreading over everything, mile after mile, thicker and
thicker to the south and west, the outfall of the volcanic
eruption. They had for some time been aware that there
was a different taste in the sea, but it hadn't been enough
to trouble them, and except in occasional pockets the tsunami and then the ordinary waves and the rains had
scoured the shoreline clean. But now, further in under
where the main plume of the eruption had been blown,
that had not been enough. When they reached the long
beach behind the water pool they found it not white but
dark gray. The beach itself had totally changed shape.
There was no water pool.

They hunted desperately for it. With the beach behind
so altered they could no longer be sure exactly where it
was supposed to be, and plunged around searching at random. It took them a long while to realize that it was in fact
gone. Perhaps the earthquakes had closed it or perhaps the
colossal shifting of sand beneath the tsunami had for the
time being blocked it off, but they didn't wonder about
causes. It was just another terrible change, part of all the
other changes. They gathered miserably in the shallows
and looked at Li.

Without her they would probably have turned back
north, in an unreasoned hope that the water caves might
somehow have come back, but Li had no such hope. The
discovery of the dolphin's body had changed her. Through
the bone she carried it seemed still to be speaking to her,
telling her that even its death was part of its song, which
she must understand. It said that there was no life for the
people anymore on this shore. They must go away, or they
too would die. The water caves were closed. The pool was
gone. When they reached the shrimping beach there

would be no glimmering harvest in the shallows, however many full moons came and went. They must go.

Where?

Li already knew the answer. There was another place. She had seen it on the day she had watched the spider, and often since then, when the tribe had been at the shrimping beach, she had crossed the dunes during the long wait between high tides, climbed into the leaning tree and looked west. Often too she had seen the place in her dreams. It was important to her because it was part of the process in which she had first become fully aware of herself, and had begun to wonder at the hugeness of the world and the otherness of all the things it held.

The retreating tsunami had left every hollow filled with salt water, but there were places where the rains that followed had collected in sufficient quantities to dilute it to a point where they could drink it, so that by the time they reached the shrimping beaches they had made up for not finding the freshwater pool. The beaches were utterly changed. The shoreline here had actually risen, so that the waves lapped far further out than they used to, and the dunes behind were no longer a series of hummocks but a single level flat, runneled where the water had coursed back toward the sea. The altered level meant that the shoreline continued ahead, with the flattened reed beds already starting to dry out. It would have been possible to continue south, looking for a new and hospitable shore, but instead Li led the way inland.

The leaning tree was gone, washed away or buried in sand and ash, but the marsh was still there, stretching away and away, and beyond it rose the line of blue hills.

Where the ground started to slope down toward the water Li stopped and pointed. The others gazed ahead, muttering surprise and doubt. Nothing stirred. The tsunami had flattened the reeds, and the rise in land level had brought the mudbanks from which they grew up above the surface, so that they lay like mats or floating islands between the patches of water. In places further out the islands seemed to join together and become a path. The water itself looked calm and safe.

Come, she said, and clutching the dolphin's blade bone to her chest, walked confidently down the slope.

Now:
Thursday
Morning

Vinny slept late. The first sound she heard was Dr. Hamiska's laugh braying through the camp. She lay for a moment, wondering how she could once have thought it was a cheerful sound. Then she remembered the first drive out to the site, when he was telling her about fossils and things. He'd been really interesting. They'd both enjoyed it. There were probably lots of people who still thought he was terrific, and from their point of view they weren't wrong. It was just sad that he'd shown Vinny his foul side.

A faint sound from inside the hut made her open her eyes. Dad was sitting at his folding table, writing. He didn't stir or twitch when the laugh rang out again. He was using his work to shut all that out, to shut everything out—Mom, May Anna, Vinny. No, wrong again. He had noticed she was awake and stopped writing.

"You've slept all right," he said.

"Yes. What's the time? Didn't you?"

"Bit after seven. No. I'm no good at quarrels. God, I'm glad it's all over. Look, Watson took the

spare jeep into town, so as soon as he gets back we'll push
off, and that means that someone can helicopter back with
the Craig people and pick it up."

"How long have we got?"

"Plenty of time. Assuming Watson didn't crash the jeep,
driving a load of girls around town, and assuming he managed to get up this morning, he should be back around
lunchtime. That'll give us just time to clear out before the
Craig people show up."

"In a helicopter!"

"They're the ones with the money. Why don't you go
and find some breakfast? I'll come when I get to a stopping
place."

He worked on steadily while Vinny dressed. Before she
left she went and stood by his chair and put her hand
around his shoulder, looking down at the neat straight lines
of his notes. His handwriting was almost as small as print,
but beautifully clear. He hesitated, wrote another couple
of lines, put his pen down, and folded his hand over hers.

"I'm glad you came," he said. "It's been a great help not
having to go through all that out there alone."

"Oh . . . Thanks, Dad. Thanks a lot."

"Go and get some breakfast."

He squeezed her hand before he picked up his pen and
started to write again.

The others had mostly finished eating, so Vinny got
herself muesli and canned milk, fruit juice, and a mango,
and ate alone. Dad, she guessed, didn't feel like facing
anyone. She could see May Anna working on her skull.
Mrs. Hamiska was talking to her. Dr. Hamiska bustled in
to the eating area, glanced around for someone, and bustled away pretending not to have noticed Vinny. He was
just like Mr. Potterson, she thought, on the day of the
school play, rushing around as if everything depended on

him and everyone would forget their lines if he weren't there.

To her surprise Mrs. Hamiska came across and sat down opposite her. Vinny said, "Good morning," and Mrs. Hamiska answered, but then sat looking at her with her head on one side as if she was trying to decide what sort of person she was. Vinny managed a few mouthfuls before she looked up. Their eyes met.

"I'm truly sorry things have turned out like this," said Mrs. Hamiska.

"It's not your fault."

"No. You know, I used rather to enjoy these academic fights. They can be almost addictive, like a drug. But now I'm tired of all that."

"I don't think there's anything anyone can do now."

"No. I'm afraid not. I've been talking to May Anna."

"It wasn't true! He wasn't trying to keep the site to himself! He wasn't trying to slow things up! He isn't like that!"

"I don't believe he is. I don't believe anyone seriously thinks that. Ah, well. I'll do my best . . . Will you tell him, please?"

"Yes, of course."

Mrs. Hamiska bowed her head and sat studying the backs of her hands. Vinny went on eating until, in a lull in the bustle of the camp, she heard a distant faint drumming sound.

"There's a helicopter," she said.

Mrs. Hamiska jerked up, startled, and listened.

"Goodness," she said. "It'll be Dr. Wishart! He must have caught an early flight! We're not nearly ready for him!"

She rose. Others had heard the sound. As it came closer they moved into the open and stood watching the sky.

Hands pointed. Vinny moved to where she could see. It was a big machine, with two rotors, and not the bright dragonfly thing which important people get ferried around in, but fat and painted in camouflage colors.

"Army chopper," said someone. "Not for us."

But it neared and neared, its racket now battering the hillside. It hovered, sank, and settled in an explosion of blown dust on the flat ground beside the truck and jeep a hundred yards down the slope. Dr. Hamiska was already loping down the path with Dr. Wessler trotting nervously behind.

A door opened. Four soldiers leapt out, guns at the ready. Then steps were lowered and a tall man wearing an embroidered pillbox hat and a long white robe came slowly down and stood between the soldiers gazing around him. Dr. Hamiska strode up with his hand outstretched in welcome, but two of the soldiers raised their guns and barred his way. He stopped, held his hands half up, and said something, protesting or questioning, but the tall man ignored him and came slowly up the path to the open space in the middle of the camp, where he stood looking proudly around him. He had a small neat beard. His face was dark brown, with rounded muscles on the cheekbones below the impenetrable black sunglasses.

He spoke at last, an order, with a gesture of the hand. One of the soldiers fetched a folding table out from under an awning and another of the group who'd followed the man up the path spread what looked like a map on it. It was at this point that Vinny saw Watson standing at the back of the group, looking for once as if he didn't specially want to be noticed.

"Where is Dr. Hamiska?" said the tall man, in English, with a strong, throaty accent.

"Here," said Dr. Hamiska calmly, as if all this were

normal. "Mr. Multan, isn't it? Honored to welcome you, Minister. How can we help you?"

He moved to face the visitor across the table. Mr. Multan gazed at him from behind his shielding glasses, obviously trying to do his own trick of facing him down, but Dr. Hamiska gazed confidently back. At length Mr. Multan tapped the map three times with his forefinger.

"You have been digging outside the area for which you have your license," he said.

"If we have, it's an oversight. Or a misunderstanding. Fetch the license, will you, Jane? Forgive me, Minister, but I believe you gave us a license covering the whole of the Dunahil district."

Mr. Multan tapped the map again, barely glancing at it as he spoke.

"This *(tap)* is the Dunahil district, here *(tap)*. Here *(tap)* is the boundary. You have been digging *(tap)* here."

Dr. Hamiska looked at the map, peered more closely, started to say something about it, stopped and straightened.

"I'm afraid it's an oversight. There wasn't a map with our license."

"That is your affair."

"In any case I would, of course, be willing to take out a fresh license to cover this outlying site, where we have, as you say, started a minor exploratory dig. I must explain, Minister, that we are expecting other visitors today, the director of the Craig Foundation, which—ah, thank you, Jane . . ."

Dr. Hamiska took the paper and was beginning to unfold it when Mr. Multan snatched it from his hands, refolded it, and tore it twice across. He dropped the pieces on the ground.

"Your license is taken away," he said. "Your visas are

taken away. You will leave the country within forty-eight hours."

"This is ridiculous . . ."

"Be silent. You think this is a tin-pot country. You think you can come here and do what you wish. You think you can take the treasures out of our soil and we will not know what you are taking, because we are savages. You think your Craig Foundation and its dollars can bribe my officials to look another way. I make it clear we are not your children, we are not your donkeys, we are not your servants. We are your equals. I ask, does it take a white man to dig a hole in the ground?"

"Color's got nothing to do with it. But it takes an expert, black or white, to know where to dig. I've worked with excellent black colleagues. Dr. Azikwe, your nephew, I think, shows every sign—"

"I am not interested in your opinion. Dr. Azikwe will now be in charge of these excavations."

"Are you serious? In that case—no, I will not be silent. Let me tell you that it's perfectly obvious to me that this so-called boundary on this map has been recently drawn in. A child could see that it's been done with a different pen, in another sort of ink—"

He stopped because a gunpoint had been thrust against his throat, but he kept his dignity as he backed away. Mr. Multan spoke with one of his aides, who came forward and clapped for attention.

"Everybody will go to his hut, please, and wait there. We are sorry for the inconvenience. We will not be very long."

"I don't understand," whispered Vinny.

Dad glanced at the door.

"It was always a risk," he muttered. "I must say I've got

a certain amount of sympathy for them. Suppose a lot of—
oh, I don't know—Martians turned up and said they
wanted to excavate a site on Salisbury Plain where several
ley lines meet, and we could have a few token humans on
the dig but we mustn't interfere because we didn't know
enough about it. How'd we feel? This country is still finding itself. For years it has been regarded as a kind of pariah
by the rest of the world. Now it can do with all the prestige
it can get, including (the Minister evidently thinks) the
prestige of taking charge of the excavation of a really important early hominid site. They've got something no one
else has got—why should they hand it all over to a pack of
Europeans and Americans?"

"But they don't know how."

"They can hire people. Fred, for a start. And I didn't say
I thought they were right, I just said . . . Hold it."

He'd been talking in a low voice, so Vinny had already
heard the approaching footsteps, but it was only Watson.
He looked almost as cocky as usual, now that he was out of
his uncle's presence.

"Hi, Vinny," he said. "Hi, Sam. Sorry about all this
happening. Didn't mean it this way."

Dad grunted unencouragingly.

"They're saying you been fired, Sam," said Watson.
"That right?"

"I have resigned over a disagreement with Dr. Hamiska,
if you must know."

"Right. Well, now you're unfired, if that's what you
want."

"What do you mean?"

"You hear the Minister saying I got to take over everything? Can't do that all by myself, you know, so I'm going
to need help. Experts. Pros. How d'you feel about that?"

"Heavens. I'll have to think. Have you asked Dr. Wessler?"

"Sooner have you, Sam. Came to you first."

"Well . . . As a matter of fact Vinny and I were planning to go on a few days' safari. Not that it looks as if that's on now."

"No problem. I'll fix it for you. You go on your trip, have a good time. I got a lot of sorting out, you know. When you come back, tell me what you think. Okay?"

"Oh . . . We were supposed to be leaving today—as soon as you got back, in fact with the jeep."

"No problem. You take the other jeep."

"You mean we can go at once?"

"Just how you like, Sam. This your bag, Vinny? Okay."

"I can't go without knowing what's happening to the others."

"They're all packing. Soldiers are bringing a truck out, taking them to the airport, putting them on a plane. Just got to go through their cases first, you know, see they're not taking anything out."

He turned to go but Vinny caught him at the door.

"Can you fix for May Anna to come with us?" she said. "If she'd like to, I mean."

"Sure. I'll be asking her to stay too. No problem."

He ambled away carrying Vinny's bag. A soldier and an official came in and went through Dad's case. They took out every scrap of paper and made him sign a receipt. When they'd finished Watson came and accompanied them down to the jeep. May Anna was already there, waiting for them.

Then

Li sat by the stream, looking out over the marsh, with the evening sun on her back. She felt exhausted but happy. They had accomplished the double journey, out to the sea for the birth of Rawi's baby and back with the child, a girl, safely born. Already the flattened reeds had sent up new shoots, as high as her waist in places. Next time a baby was born they would be an impenetrable barrier. A new way would have to be found.

Rawi had been very restless before the birth, begging the others to come with her, making short forays into the marsh alone, returning and begging again. In the end Ma-ma had agreed to go with her, so Li had gone too and the rest had followed.

It had been a good birth, at dawn in the shallows below the shrimping beaches, and they had stayed there till evening, not wishing to recross the marshes in the heat of the day. The moon had been almost full when they had crossed the night before, so at noon they shrimped experimentally below the old beaches, and to their amazed delight had caught a few transparent wrigglers. Even so there had been

no question of their staying for the midnight tide. The
stream was now their home, and they must get back there.

So they had returned, and feasted in the dawn off young
chicks raided from the tens of thousands of nests among
the fresh-grown reeds. Immense flocks of migrant birds
used the marshes as a breeding place. It was this that had
saved their lives when they had reached the stream after
that first terrifying journey from the sea. Practically all the
life of the marsh—the birds already there, the fish, the
crocodiles, the pigs—had been killed by the outfall from
the eruption, and then the tsunami, but fresh flocks had
already arrived and, having nowhere else to go, had started
to nest and lay among the flattened reed beds, so at least
there had been eggs. The water of the marsh had been salt
from the tsunami, and sulfurous from the volcano, but the
stream they had reached ran from somewhere far inland
and was fresh and sweet. All around, everywhere, as far as
they could see, the landscape had been the same dead
ashen gray. It had seemed at first an impossible place to
live. But, just as for the birds, there had been nowhere else.

Between an evening and a morning the marsh had
turned green as the first reed shoots showed. Li watched a
spider building a web between the twigs of a dead bush
that stood beside the stream. The stream itself scoured its
bed clean and there were shellfish there, freshwater mussels
and a clamlike thing, most of them dead and gaping,
poisoned by the fallout, but a few still sound. The area of
the marsh where the fresh water spread out started to
swarm with minnows. Bugs of various kinds appeared.
And here and there across the hills pockets of flowers
bloomed, their seeds germinating in response to the second rains and the stems managing to struggle through the
layer of ash where it happened to lie more thinly than
elsewhere.

On the morning of their return after the birth of Rawi's baby she came to Li with a *Beseech* gesture and gave her a clamshell with a shiny inner surface, then tugged appealingly at strands of her own hair. Presh was dead, so there was no father to bring gifts of food, or the birth ornament, but Rawi still longed for one. Li took the shell and turned it over in her hands, thinking. It wouldn't work without a hole.

She gathered a handful of shells from the stream bed and began experimenting. To open a living shellfish you laid it on a rock and bashed it with a flat stone. That was no good. The empty shells simply splintered. A pointed stone, then. She found one and bashed with that, but it was still no good. She was trying pure pressure when the stone slipped and the shell shot away, but starting again she noticed that she had actually managed to scratch the surface. If she could scratch and scratch and scratch . . . After many experiments she discovered a technique of pressing the point down hard with one hand and twisting the shell to and fro beneath it. The process took a long while, but it worked in the end, and by evening Rawi was wearing her ornament, content.

So now Li was sitting on the boulder around which the stream curled just before it reached the marsh and watching a vast flock of new strange birds which were paddling on stilted legs between the reed beds. Beyond them the faint layers of mist were starting to rise and spread. The world, she felt, was full of interest, and wonder, and promise. The birth of Rawi's daughter was as wonderful as anything, because it showed that despite all the changes and horrors things were well, things were as they were meant to be.

Something had made all this happen, on purpose, just as she, Li, had made the hole in Rawi's shell. Something had caused her to be sitting on this rock, this very evening, herself, Li. She felt that she was being watched with the same intentness as she had watched the spider building its web long ago under the leaning tree above the shrimping beaches, or the other spider only a few days back. Yes, like that, that sort of web, herself at the center of it, all the lines drawing in to her, here, now. No one else. Nowhere else. No other time.

It was the dolphins, she knew. They were still with her, still her friends and helpers, wherever they seemed to have gone. One day she would go there too, and dance with them again in their golden seas where the sun was born, and learn the meaning of their song.

She picked up the shoulder blade from beside her and studied it, turning it to and fro in the evening sunlight. She had carried it now so long that it seemed part of her, so much so that not having it in her hand made her feel strange, but it would be better if she could wear it on a loop of hair, like a birth ornament. Then she would always have both hands free. It was much thicker than the shell, but not so hard. She would need to be very careful. There would be no way of finding another one if she broke it.

She chose a place near one corner, adjusted the bone onto a jut of rock, pressed the point of the stone she had used for Rawi's shell firmly down and with her other hand began to slowly turn the bone.

Now: Thursday Afternoon

They broke the journey to rest in the shade of a flat-topped tree beside the track. There were no weaver-bird nests in it, but otherwise it could have been the same one where Dad and Vinny had stopped for lunch five days ago, just one tree in the enormous plain which had once been sea. The sun was halfway down the burning sky.

The buzz of a helicopter came faintly from the northwest, louder as it neared until they saw it race by about half a mile away, an ordinary commercial machine painted scarlet and silver. Dad laughed.

"Bet that's Wishart on his way to the camp," he said. "His flight must have been late. He's in for a shock."

"What'll happen?" said Vinny.

"Lord knows. The Minister's still there, unless he's gone home by another route. I don't think Joe's going to be able to make it up with him. Wishart is a thoroughly nasty piece of work, in my opinion. I've only met him once, and he struck me as both prickly and slippery. I doubt if he'll hit it off with the Minister."

"Fred will be loving all this," said May Anna.

"I think Fred's going to come out on top," said Dad. "He's got the contacts Watson needs. If we've got what we think we have, he'll be able to raise the funds . . ."

"Aren't you going to help?" said Vinny. "Watson's not too bad, honestly he isn't . . ."

"Just think what Joe would make of it," said Dad. "I set all this up in order to lever him out and take over. The mere fact that Watson promptly arranged for us to keep our visas . . . No, I'm going to look for something with a bit less hassle in it than hominids. There's plenty of interesting work to be done. What about you, May Anna?"

"I told Watson I'll come back. I want to finish my skull. It's getting really interesting. It's got some fascinating features—clearly hominid, but so small. Male, I think. And, do you know, something fractured it, just behind the left temple. No, seriously."

"You're as bad as Joe," said Dad.

He laughed, then sighed.

"I'd like to have finished it," he said. "Let's pray Watson manages to keep control of things and get the material into some kind of decent storage. I can just see those soldiers shoveling them into plastic bags and slinging them into some corner, and then . . . You know they took every scrap of my notes?"

"Mine too," said May Anna. "All gone."

"I've still got my bone," said Vinny.

"What bone?" said May Anna.

"A scapula she was drawing," said Dad. "Hang on— let's think about this. Didn't they go through your bag?"

"Watson carried it out to the jeep, remember."

"Oh, Lord. Look, I'm afraid we're going to have to dispose of it for the moment. I'm still a bit jumpy about someone going through our bags again, and we certainly can't risk taking it out."

"If May Anna's going back . . ." said Vinny.

"The trouble is there's no documentation," said Dad. "There's nothing in my notes."

"If she just put it back in the H bag," said Vinny. "Then perhaps someone could notice . . . *you* could notice, May Anna . . ."

"Please," said May Anna.

Dad laughed.

"See what you think. Show her, Vinny. Don't say anything."

Vinny fetched the fossil and gave it to May Anna, who studied it first with the naked eye and then through a magnifying glass, tilting it this way and that in a patch of sunlight to reveal its faint markings.

"Someone's bored a hole here," she said.

"Possibly," said Dad.

"Not just possibly. Look. There's these drill scratches this side, and look at the wearing this side. They've pressed down onto it with a pointed flake, using a rock as an anvil, but they didn't turn the flake. They turned the scapula. If you didn't have a fully manipulable hand and wrist, you'd find that easier. You're telling me this came from your site?"

"Out of the H layer. The one with the foot bones in it," said Vinny.

May Anna whistled.

"And you didn't tell Joe?" she said.

"It was tricky," said Dad. "By the time Vinny noticed those scratch marks—I told you she was drawing it—we were already having trouble with him."

"It was my fault," said Vinny. "I asked Dad not to tell

him. I hated the way he kept making a fuss, pretending I was his lucky mascot and so on."

"It was partly that," said Dad. "Anyway, I wasn't as sure as you are about the significance of those scratches—in fact I'm still not. Furthermore, if you're right, then it's going to cast considerable doubt on our dating. You're not going to get a lot of paleontologists believing in an artifact four and a half million years old, for a start."

May Anna sat silent, still turning the bone to and fro.

"What do you think it is?" said Vinny. "I mean, what sort of animal did it come from? Dad doesn't know."

"Just what I was thinking about. Were you ever at Pechabar, Sam?"

"Remind me."

"It was the first real site I worked on. Pakistan. Harry Blakey ran it. It was amazing, a sort of cetacean graveyard. There must have been one almighty stranding incident. When I was still a student I'd handled more cetacean fossils than most guys see in a lifetime. That's whales and dolphins, Vinny."

"I know. It would be neat if it was a dolphin."

"What on earth do you mean 'neat'?" said Dad. "I can't think of anything more untidy than an early hominid drilling a hole in a dolphin scapula."

"We came from the sea, Dad. Like I keep telling you."

He laughed cheerfully and hardly at all with scorn, and May Anna joined in.

"You haven't cured her of that bug yet, Sam?" she said.

"It isn't a bug," said Vinny. "You said you didn't think it was complete nonsense. I bet you really think there might be something in it!"

"Me? A poor girl with a career to make? I can't afford to . . . What do you want me to do, Sam?"

"Do you think you could find this tree again?"

May Anna looked around, checking landmarks.

"Sure," she said.

"Then I think we'll bury it here for the moment. When you get back—if you get back—you can check out how things are. Maybe you'll simply be able to tell Watson what happened. Maybe you'll be able to sneak it into the H bag somehow. Maybe things won't work out and it'll have to stay here. If necessary I can send you a note about it once I'm out of the country. All right?"

So they measured a distance from the trunk and hacked a good deep hole and wrapped the fossil in plastic and laid it in the bottom and stamped the earth back firm above it. Vinny rose dizzy from bending and stood and swayed with the world dark and her ears drumming. It was strange knowing where the fossil was hidden, and knowing that she and Dad and May Anna were the only ones in all the world who had that knowledge. It gave her a sudden sense of her own uniqueness, her singleness, as if she were a particular point where various lines, drawn right across the universe, came together, focusing here, now.

The drumming left her and her vision cleared. Around her the plain which had once been sea stretched into its unknowable wavering distances, like time.

Note

There were apes, walking on four legs, and millions of years later there were our human ancestors, walking on two. What happened in those millions of years to bring that about is still largely guesswork.

The sea-ape theory is one of those guesses. Professional paleontologists have tended to call it crackpot, but some of them are beginning to agree that it at least needs a serious answer. Vinny mentions some of the arguments for it: our hairlessness, the fat beneath our skins, our hearts slowing when we dive, and so on. The chief arguments against it are that there aren't any fossils and there doesn't seem to be enough time to fit that amount of evolution in. I would like to have written more about it, but I found it held the story up too much. Readers who are interested should look for Elaine Morgan's books, *The Descent of Woman* and *The Aquatic Ape*.

I have, of course, made up everything that Li and her people do in this story. There's no evidence for that at all.

P.D.

About the Author

Peter Dickinson was born in what is now Zambia. He is the author of many distinguished books for children and adults. In Britain his novels for children have received several awards, among them the Carnegie Medal for *Tulku* and for *City of Gold,* the *Guardian* Award for *The Blue Hawk,* and the Whitbread Award for *Tulku* and, most recently, for *AK.* In America his novel *Eva* was an ALA Best Book for Young Adults and was named the *Boston Globe/Horn Book* Honor Book in Fiction for 1989.

Peter Dickinson lives in London.

1381 1764